The Lost Child of Lychford

ALSO BY PAUL CORNELL

Witches of Lychford
British Summertime
Something More
A Better Way to Die (collection)

THE SHADOW POLICE SERIES
London Falling
The Severed Streets
Who Killed Sherlock Holmes?

THE LOST CHILD
OF LYCHFORD

PAUL CORNELL

A TOM DOHERTY ASSOCIATES BOOK

NEW YORK

This is a work of fiction. All of the characters, organization, and events portrayed in this novella are either products of the author's imagination or are used fictitiously.

THE LOST CHILD OF LYCHFORD

Copyright © 2016 by Paul Cornell

Cover photograph by Getty Images
Cover design by FORT

Edited by Lee Harris

A Tor.com Book
Published by Tom Doherty Associates
175 Fifth Avenue
New York, NY 10010

www.tor.com

Tor® is a registered trademark of Macmillan Publishing Group, LLC.

ISBN 978-0-7653-8976-3 (ebook)
ISBN 978-0-7653-8977-0 (trade paperback)

First Edition: November 2016

The Lost Child of Lychford

1

The Reverend Lizzie Blackmore slowly blinked awake, and found, to her surprise, that she was already furious. She was furious as if she'd been angry in her dreams, oppressed and confined by something she couldn't recall, and waking up was just one more damned thing. But why? It must be the sound, she decided, an irritating, whiny sound that was wheedling itself into her brain and then poking it.

She looked over at her clock radio and swore at it. "It's still two weeks to Christmas, and you're playing Greg Lake?!"

———

"The song 'I Believe in Father Christmas,'" she continued to Sue and Oliver, her elderly churchwardens, twelve hours later, at their weekly meeting round the vicarage kitchen table, "should be banned. It should be a crime to play it. What else has he recorded? 'Valentine's Day Is Just to Sell Cards'? 'Look Out for Wasps, It's Summer'?

Radio stations only play it because it's got that nice bit with the jingle bells, but he's doing that *sarcastically*. He's doing *sarcastic* jingle bells."

"I did like him in Crosby, Stills and Nash," opined Oliver, who knew what he meant.

"Wow," said Sue. "We're still two weeks out. And you're already that far gone."

Lizzie realised the two of them were looking at her with newfound wariness. This was going to be her first Christmas as vicar of St. Martin's church, Lychford. The churchwardens, however, had a long experience of working with her predecessor. All vicars had a rough time of it at Christmas, but she was obviously setting off their alarm bells already. "Chris de Burgh can sod off as well," she said. "And I liked The Pogues the first eighty-nine times, but come on. Anyway, why are we talking about this? We've got a lot to do. Can we please get on?"

They did indeed have a lot to do. Lizzie most of all. She'd expected to feel daunted. She'd spent the year trying to attract new members into the congregation, and Christmas was traditionally the time when a whole bunch of people who wouldn't otherwise cross the threshold of a church came piling in. The challenge was to somehow keep them afterwards, while running an ecclesiastical assault course. She'd already gotten over the first few hurdles of the season. The Advent Carol Service, which she'd insisted that this year was going to be by candlelight—despite Oliver's misgivings that this would result in what he called a "*Towering Inferno* scenario"—had turned out to actually be problematic in other ways. Lizzie had had to lead the plainsong while not being able to see anything. The congregation attracted by the poster hadn't really sung along, and, as they filed out, Lizzie found them to be a bit bemused that the songs they'd just awkwardly picked their way through were what the Anglican Communion regarded as "carols." "I like 'Silent Night,'" one young woman had said, "but perhaps that's a bit too popular for you." Lizzie had nearly replied there was a little number by Greg Lake she'd probably enjoy.

Then there had been Christingle, which had meant more fire—and this time children were handling it—and which brought in very few people who understood why there were oranges with candles stuck in them. At times, Lizzie had wondered if the best way to deal with the added numbers might be some sort of video prologue. "Previously, in Christianity . . ."

But what she was feeling went beyond daunted, beyond useless, beyond stressed. There was a sort of . . . background anger, a feeling of being downtrodden. She really didn't understand it, and it was getting in the way of what should be a season of joy. That's what Christmas had always been for her in the past.

The morning after the churchwardens' meeting, she went into the church to check the stocks of wine, wafers, and hymn sheets, ready for the forthcoming onslaught. There were fourteen more days of frantic organisation and hopefully passionate delivery ahead of her, as well as all the other matters of life and death which, in the normal course of parish life, kept her really pretty damn busy. On top of all that was the sombre fact that Christmas killed people. Old folk tried to hang on for one last Christmas lunch and found that took a bit too much out of them. Or just about managed to hold on, but then immediately expired. So she had a larger number of funerals than usual to attend to as well.

And still, beyond all that—the star atop Lizzie's personal Christmas tree of stress—there was the wedding. For the last few months, she'd been meeting with a couple from Swindon who were deluded enough to believe that to get married on Christmas Eve was to be the stars of one's own festive rom com. She'd tried to dissuade them, saying spring was so much nicer. She'd pointed out that other parishes were available. She'd shown them just how many other services she had to fit in on that day. She'd shown them around the church, pointing out how small and drafty it was. But no. They were set on it. So that was yet another damn thing.

On the way to the vestry, she dipped before the altar, stopping a moment to recheck the Advent dressings placed on it. The low light through the windows gave the building an air of quiet contemplation. She wished she felt the same.

She heard a noise from behind her.

She turned and saw, standing some distance away, a child. It was a boy of about three years old. He had his back to her, his arms by his sides, looking at the ancient map of Lychford and its surroundings which was once again on display and featured on the list of points of interest in the church's tourist leaflet.

This was a bit odd. There'd been nobody on the path outside, and she was pretty sure there was nobody else in the building. "Hi," she called.

He didn't reply.

Lizzie walked down the length of the church towards him, not wanting to scare him. As she approached, she heard he was muttering to himself, in the way toddlers did. "Say hello, everybody."

"Hello," said Lizzie again. She'd put on her brightest voice. She didn't want him running away. She realised that, oddly, some part of her was also feeling . . . afraid. There was something not quite right about . . . what?

The boy turned to look at her. His expression wasn't the excited interest you normally expected from a child of that age. It was a look of terrible, lost pain. It was an expression that should only appear on a much older face.

Since having the waters of the well in the woods thrown over her by Judith Mawson, Lizzie had seen some extraordinary things. She could now sense what those who lived in the everyday streets of Lychford seldom saw, the effects and creatures of . . . she hated to use the word, but of magic. She realised now that here she was seeing something else of that world. This little boy wasn't quite here. She realised that, now she was up close, she could see through him.

This was her first ghost.

The feeling was almost one of relief. That this wasn't a real child who demanded her immediate care, but one for whom that care was . . . too late? But no. Here he was, right in front of her, his expression demanding . . . something. This was no Victorian urchin. This boy had a Thomas the Tank Engine pullover, and those tiny trainers with lights on them.

"Not Mummy," the boy said. "Where's Mummy?"

"Are your Mum and Dad about?" she said, helplessly. Did she expect there to be a ghost Mum and Dad? Wouldn't that be cosy?

"No hurting," he said. It was half a plea, half scolding.

He was literally radiating anxiety, a coldness she could feel on her skin. Lizzie squatted down and reached out to him, encouraging him to come to her. He backed away. She was scaring him. Was it just because she wasn't his Mummy? A second later, without any sense of movement, he was gone.

Lizzie got slowly to her feet. She realised she was shaking. She herself had never wanted to be a mother, but the way that small boy had needed *someone,* to get him back to where he should be, wherever that was—

She jumped at the sound of the church door opening.

It was Sue, carrying an armful of candles. "Sorry," she said. "Hope I didn't disturb you."

———

"It's probably not real," said Judith, who was sitting exactly where Lizzie had expected to find her, behind the counter of Witches: The Magic Shop. These days, the old lady seemed only to venture away from her post among the potions and unicorn figurines and crystal balls to reluctantly head home, and that was often late in the evening. The elderly witch complained bitterly, to anyone who'd listen, about her new situation as a "shop girl," but spent so much time in that shop that Lizzie could only think she protested too much.

"Those are not words I ever expected to hear you say," said Lizzie, who'd been relieved to have had provided for her a cup one of the shop's more soothing herbal teas.

"Well, of course it's a bloody *ghost*. Your church *is* haunted."

"So by 'not real' you mean . . . ?"

"A ghost isn't often a person. It most probably don't have feelings you can hurt or soothe. It's just a . . . whatchamacallit, a symbol. Like the green man on the traffic light."

Lizzie tried to get her head around the idea that that frightened little boy might appear in her church as often as the sign at the pedestrian crossing turned green. "So . . . is it sort of an architectural feature, a recording of something that happened, or is it there because . . . ?" *Because of me,* she wanted to say. Where had that thought come from?

Autumn, who owned the shop, and was, as always, dressed as if she'd staggered out of an explosion in Next, brought the pot of tea over, a concerned expression on her face. "Ah, now, wait. I've read a lot of texts that say ghosts are the souls of people who are prevented from getting into heaven—"

"I don't believe anything *could* prevent them," said Lizzie. "If there *is* a heaven, about which Biblical sources—"

"—but I was about to add," finished Autumn pointedly, "that since I don't believe in an afterlife, I don't think that can be true."

"It's not like there's a vote on what's real," said Judith. "It don't matter what either of you believe, the world just gets on with it. Still, at least you're agreeing on summat, which is that it's probably not real either way. Might be a recording, like you say. Might be summat else."

"However," Autumn stressed, "I'm trying to train Judith in the correct approach to customers, and, Lizzie Bizzie, you are, at this moment, a customer."

"I haven't bought anything," said Lizzie, feeling now vaguely as if she should.

Autumn ignored her. "Judith, what have I told you about addressing the feelings of customers first, before getting into the details of why they're visiting us?"

Judith glowered. "Summat annoying, I should think."

"I *am* paying you to work here."

"Only because you're now *my* apprentice and you want me here so *you* can learn from *me*."

"You still have to actually do the job. And I'm trying to teach you how. We have a Christmas rush on." Autumn gestured at the empty shop, completely without irony. "It's time you learned about customer satisfaction."

Judith carefully took out her hanky, spat into it in disgust, then put it back in her pocket, as if this were the epitome of etiquette.

"Well, this has been informative," said Lizzie, just as exasperated by the impossible situation these two had set up for themselves as she had been on the last few occasions she'd visited. It was always good to see her friends, but it wasn't as if they could understand her situation, when Autumn still sometimes referred to Lizzie only working on Sundays. And now they'd used her child ghost as just the basis for another row. She made her good-byes, threw her scarf round her neck, and just about managed to avoid slamming the door.

———————

That evening, Judith Mawson left the shop rather earlier than usual, and headed up to the marketplace, then up the road to St. Martin's churchyard. At the start of December, the church had had a neon star put on the top of its tower. Now Judith looked up at it and snorted. "Bloody Christmas," she said. She couldn't be having with the sort of uncontainable, overexcited enthusiasm the Reverend Lizzie displayed for such a tiring season. She pushed herself forward on her stick and headed for the church door.

Judith knew there were at least a dozen things a ghost could be, including, well, she didn't like to call such things souls, that being ecclesiastical territory, but yes, summat that was still a person. She didn't like being vague to just about the only two individuals in this town it was possible that in a few years' time she'd get round to calling friends. However, there existed a worrying possibility about what this was, and she didn't want to burden Lizzie with that thought until she was sure. It was possible that the Reverend had been cursed. Perhaps not with ... something as personal as Judith's own burden, but certainly with something that had scared her, badly. Despite her trying so hard to be Ms. Vicar and not show it. Bloody Autumn had, of course, remained oblivious. But the wise woman had seen.

Judith tried the door, found it to be still unlocked, and stepped into the empty church. She sniffed the air. Nothing she hadn't expected. The flavour of the air was slightly different, as churches always got at this time of year, as different belief systems crowded in. Was that something sinister, right at the bottom of the range? Probably just the occasional deeply unrighteous individual, only to be expected in a big crowd. A village witch like her was always a bit lost when presented with people in numbers. She put that thought aside and addressed the air. "Right, then," she called out, "what are you?"

She didn't really expect an answer. Not in words. The tone of her voice had been calculated, through experience, to reach whatever had started roosting in this place.

There was, in reply, just a slight movement of air.

It was hiding from her. Through fear or malice? Not sure. Judith tasted the air once more. She knew things that had been born out there in the dark beyond the bounds of the town that could conceal themselves, could even lie about their natures, but she knew most of the flavours of that deceit.

She was startled to suddenly find a new flavour on her taste buds. This wasn't something that was ... here ... as such, this was a connection to something somewhere else. She flexed her old fingers painfully and drew it out of the air in more detail, rubbing it between her numb fingertips. She grew worried at what she felt. There *was* something of it that reminded her of Lizzie. So there was an association between the Reverend and this child, not a curse, but it was ... complicated. Mixed-up. It would need a working of magic to explore in more detail.

To Judith's surprise, the ghost now appeared, looking at her from around the edge of a pew. That lost, demanding face. Judith looked sternly back. Yes, she could see how that would get to the soft girl. "You go on home, then," she said. It had come out more gently than she'd intended. "If you know where that is. I give you permission to do so and I give you strength." She winced as the little pulse of life left her. She hadn't meant to give up so much of that either. She'd regret that moment on her deathbed.

However, the thing didn't collapse into cold air, as she expected it to. It just kept looking mournfully at her, and then, as if it had decided she couldn't provide it with whatever it was seeking, it once more faded.

Judith found she had a catch in her throat. Half of it was that she felt tricked. Half of it was that it was the oldest trick of all. The trick of affection. She was getting soft herself. "Stupid old woman," she whispered to herself as she left the church. "Stupid."

———

"Stupid," said Autumn to herself, sitting at the PC in the room above the shop that doubled as her office and bedroom. Her finger was hovering over the "delete profile" button on a dating website. It had been hovering there for about a minute now, as she watched the number of messages coming in increase. Twice in that minute she'd taken a quick glance at those messages. Both times she'd gone right back to wanting to delete the whole thing. The genius of this site, she realised, was the bait of hope. One of the men trying desperately to contact her might turn out to be able to string a sentence together, one that wasn't immediately blunt or abusive. She felt she had somehow let herself down in having ventured to this online location, to the realm of the desperate and deranged. Christmas always did this to her. It emphasised how alone she was. There were, as far as Autumn could work out, exactly two single men of around her age in Lychford. She ran into them every now and then down the Plough. One of them seemed only interested in her as a possible cleaning lady, the other—though in this town he was probably never going to admit it even to himself—would only ever be interested in her as a shoulder to cry on. The other possibility was for her to get herself out to the bright lights of Swindon or Cirencester; but the idea of getting done up, then driving alone to stand in some bar, not even being able to have more than one glass of wine to give one an excuse for being there, while the contents of this dating site sloshed around the room in person . . . She stood up, not liking the direction her thoughts were going, and had to take a quick walk around the room. It was either that or throw the PC out of the window. How did anyone ever meet anyone? How was it the human race hadn't gone extinct? Jolly thoughts for Yuletide.

She felt relief, therefore, at the *bing* of an incoming email, and sat down again to open it, hoping it was from Lizzie, who she really should talk to about all this; only it was coming up to Christmas, so she'd be busy for at least a couple of days every week, and Autumn didn't want to spoil how joyful the season seemed to be making her friend, except . . . now that Autumn thought about it, it seemed that Lizzie had actually been freaked out to a weird degree by seeing that ghost. As if it hadn't been just one of those things that those who had their gift had to get used to, but was . . . personal somehow. Well, that would give her a good excuse to visit and share their worries over some wine. How about she just went over there right—

She stopped as she saw who the email was from, at a service provider's address which . . . no, even if she squinted, she couldn't quite read it. It was like her screen couldn't handle the language it was written in, so it didn't matter whether or not her newly empowered eyes could have deciphered the original. Her new senses, incidentally, had only added to her dating problems, because now some of the men she encountered came with added visual baggage that was literally hanging around their necks, and—

"Would you please just bloody read me?" said the email.

Autumn leapt back in her chair. A voice had actually come from her computer. A horribly familiar voice. Then the face associated with that voice appeared, looking out of the corner of her screen, incarnated as a cartoon version of himself. "You seem," said Finn, "to be having trouble opening an email. Can I help with that?"

"No you bloody can't. What are you doing inside my computer? Here, can you see my downloads?"

"I'm only 'inside your computer' in the sense that I'm an email. Can an email see inside your computer? Hey, what's in here, anyhow?"

Autumn was in no way going to answer that. She'd once got very drunk with Lizzie and started talking about her very specific tastes in fan fiction, and thank God the Reverend had claimed in the morning not to remember a thing. "How do I get you out of there?"

"Well, if you click on the email—"

Autumn, not being able to stand his patronising tone any longer, did so before he'd finished the sentence. To her surprise, the cartoon figure leapt out of the screen and became his real, solid self. Well, as close to solid as Finn, Prince of the Blood, from a land Judith sometimes called "where the Fairies live," could get.

"—then," he finished, "I will appear."

Autumn pulled her dressing gown tighter. "If I'd known you were going to appear—"

"You would have known, if you'd let me finish my—"

"And what are you doing here, anyway? I haven't seen you since—"

"I have been deliberately staying away, not infringing

on your boundaries. I mean both those of Lychford and your own personal ones. Since you three got together and reinforced all the borders, my lot have slept a lot more soundly. So there wasn't any urgent need for me to come and see you. Besides, since I became aware of it last time round, I've gotten a taste for this Internet thing—"

"You're on the Internet? You've got a computer?"

"Yes and no, in that order. I tasted it when I came here last time, so reached under the border and started swigging it from the air." He made a gesture as if he were drinking a pint. "And that's when it dawned on me: the menfolk you have in this world are shite."

Autumn cocked her head to one side. "Oh," she said, "what an extraordinary revelation. Mind blown."

"Yeah!" He nodded excitedly. "I knew if I pointed it out, you'd be quick to see it. You're clever like that. And when I was drinking in the Internet, I saw everything they're doing to ladies, all at once, and I was horrified. And then turned on, quite a lot. And then horrified again . . . when I realised I should be. Because last time out, I behaved a bit like that to you. By accident, largely. And that's when I decided to stay away entirely. To avoid doing that again."

Autumn stared at him. Oh God, he was serious. It wasn't like she'd wanted him to stay away. She thought they'd gotten things sorted out. Although a bit of her was pleased that just for once *she'd* managed to freak *him* out. He wasn't going to be all guilty and try to sympathise his way into her affections now, was he? She shook her head. He was running her in circles already. "You could just . . . avoid doing that again. Whatever it was."

"I could." He nodded.

She waited for the other shoe to drop, but as always with Finn, it failed to. It was like he only wore one shoe. "So . . . if you'd decided to stay away, why are you actually . . . back?"

She'd half expected him to be affronted by that, but he kept with the serious. "Because something's going terribly wrong. With reality, I mean. Listen, let me tell you everything. In the form of three songs and a list."

"Could you maybe just—?"

"The list summarises the songs. As always, I've thought of everything."

The next morning Lizzie went, as she did on the same morning every week, to stand by the gates of Jonathan Canter, the Lychford school of which she was an ex officio governor, and welcome parents and children as they blocked the roads for miles around. Jonathan Canter, Sue often said, was the main reason for the bypass. The churchwarden had known the man the school was named after, back in the day, a local property magnate whose trust still owned a lot of local land, particularly, it seemed, anywhere Lizzie and her team might want to expand the burial grounds into. That his lasting memorial was traffic congestion would, Sue said, have delighted him.

Lizzie hadn't slept very well the previous night. Months ago she'd taken the pillows from the other side of her bed, put furniture on the side of the room that she associated with her deceased partner, and managed to find a sort of college dorm room ambience that had allowed her to rest. Before the stress of the last few weeks. Now she couldn't get the face of that little boy out of her head. It was like he was demanding something urgent of her, and she should know what it was all about, but she didn't. She made herself be attentive as she said hello to the incoming mass of children, and had a couple of conversations with parents about baptisms and the weather and how lovely it was that Christmas was approaching, and wasn't it nice that The Pogues and, yes, there we go, Greg Lake were back in the charts, and it must be getting so busy for her, now that she had to work for most of the week. Lizzie found she was searching the children's faces as their breath billowed around them in the frosty air, mentally matching the little boy's expression with their hopeful ones, all of them full of Christmas. Full of the thought of presents and food, that was. Full of what money was doing to them and the world they lived in. She shouldn't be thinking like this, she knew, when she should be full of—

She realised she was looking right at him.

She was looking at him, the boy from the church; there he was, looking right back at her!

He was standing hand in hand with what must have been his mother as she, and what must have been his elder sister beside her, talked to Roz, the deputy headmistress. The boy had a quizzical expression on his face. He was wondering why she was staring, she realised. It was definitely the same child. He was even wearing the same pullover and shoes. Only he had none of that cold loneliness about him. There was nothing her newfound senses found odd about him at all. This was no ghost. This boy was flesh and blood.

Lizzie must have made a sound. The boy's mother looked round. Lizzie briefly considered what she could say, what she could ask. The mother had long brown hair, was in her early thirties, harassed and loving, also utterly normal. Lizzie decided the best thing she could do was to turn her expression of sudden horror into a cough. Which allowed her to strike up the briefest of conversations with Allison Dunning, as the boy's mother turned out to be called, about how there was a lot of it going around.

As Allison led the boy away, Lizzie kept staring after him, and he looked back, seemingly as puzzled about her as she was about him.

———————

"Like I said," Judith maintained, poker-faced, from her perch at the Witches till, "not real."

"He's an actual, living child, Jamie Dunning, goes to nursery at Magic Carpet. How much more real can you get?" Lizzie was pacing, having not been offered tea, since Autumn was still apparently busy upstairs. Lizzie had come running here, when actually she should be doing a host of things related to her actual job. Because this felt somehow more important.

"I mean what's in your church isn't a real ghost. It's an apparition of the living. A doppelgänger."

"Trouble," said Autumn, entering from the stairwell.

"They can be," said Judith. "They're usually either a warning of an approaching event, an attempt to stop it from coming to pass, or, when they're playing nasty buggers, something that can cause that event to happen, a self-fulfilling prophecy."

"I mean," said Autumn, before Lizzie could ask her

urgent questions, "we've got trouble with the borders. Something's trying to sneak over. I've been ... communing with the fairies."

"Have you really?" Lizzie asked, unable to stop herself from placing a rather adolescent emphasis on the last word of that sentence.

"And he sends his regards," said Autumn. "He says his people can feel a sort of ... shakiness to the boundaries, as if something's messing up the system. He provided me with this list of points of where they've felt things are getting weird."

Judith took the piece of paper and tutted at it. "Bloody fairy geography. They have no idea how to talk to us about where things are."

"And that's the translated version. You should have heard the songs. Anyway, he said they can't work out what's going on, and so, without consulting his father or anyone else, or so he says, Finn came to me to get us involved."

"They'd never be seen to ask for help from humans," said Judith. "Not as a nation. Not directly. He's actually been sent by his father to get us onside, and he wouldn't have been unless ..." She paused. "As a mere employee, am I allowed to swear in your shop?"

"You've been swearing all the bloody time."

"I mean *really* swear?"

"Why would you want to swear?" asked Lizzie. "What have you just thought of?"

"The doppelgänger in your church might have been caused by some enormous trauma of the borders, the map being shaken up by something. Time sometimes gets muddled up a bit when that happens. And since there's some connection between you and the ghost . . . oh, I found out there was. Should have told you before, I suppose." She held up a hand to once again stop Lizzie's questions. "That's all I know. It's something that's going to take a bit of biting down into. We should walk the bounds tonight."

———————————

These days, Lizzie found the woods that surrounded the town to be in equal parts beautiful and fearful, especially at night. As she kept a slow pace to match that of Judith on the path that went under the bridge and up into the trees, the taste of the air spoke of forthcoming snow. Autumn was wrapped up in a fake fur that looked like something Marianne Faithfull would have rocked in the 1960s. On anyone else it would have been white, but somehow her friend's way with clothing had touched it, and there were hints of reds and purples. Autumn was wearing the sort of frown that Lizzie usually associated with her arriving on the doorstep in the early hours. Whenever the subject of Finn came up, there was a flash of that look. She herself was still full of worrying questions, but she'd already had all the answers she could get. Part of her feared those answers.

It was already dark by the time they got up to the ridge the locals called Maiden Hill. There was now a new line of a few saplings, still fenced off, but the trees weren't yet tall enough to obscure the view of the town. A half moon was rising over the vale, with a few scudding clouds illuminated by it. Below lay Lychford, the shape of it made visible by the lights: the cross of compass-pointing roads that met in the marketplace; the church off to one side, with alignments of its own; the new developments of the Backs blossoming out; the river the artery that ran through all of it. In the dark, the town was like a cluster of small fires that spoke of hearth and comfort, that should speak to her, Lizzie knew underneath it all, of Christmas. She wished she could find that feeling.

But here she was with her two friends, who would now always be kept by the burden of their knowledge at a little distance from that warmth. This is where the three "witches" would always be. They needed to be out here looking over it in order to protect it. Did that distance add to how she was feeling? "And you don't get proper Christmas Number Ones these days," she said.

"Just whoever's won the bloody *X Factor*."

Judith looked at her and blinked like a tortoise. "What does that have to do with anything?"

"She does this," said Autumn. "She continues conversations like the eight conversations in between haven't happened."

Judith considered them both for a moment, then made a noise in the back of her throat and marched off.

Lizzie was about to follow when Autumn put a hand on her arm. "Are you okay?"

Lizzie didn't know where to begin. Now was not the time. "I'm fine."

"Come on, this is me. It always takes me a while to realise, but I always get there. And it's not like Judith's ever going to notice."

Lizzie sighed. She always appreciated Autumn's moments of empathic clarity, but this time her concern just seemed to add to the awkwardness she felt. "If I'm not fine, I don't know why. I mean . . . that little boy is absolutely not dead. I've made a few discrete inquiries about him. He's got a loving family, no trouble at home."

"But—?"

Lizzie hated the way Autumn could always do that. Her rare moments of understanding tended to go all the way. "But he doesn't . . . feel right. He feels like he's asking something of me. Or . . . blaming me for something."

"What, like the two ghosts in *The Muppet Christmas Carol*?"

"Or just the one in *A Christmas Carol*, yes."

"But what would he be blaming you for?"

Lizzie really had no idea. That was where the void was. She felt guilty without knowing what she'd done. She just shook her head. At that moment, thankfully, Judith called to them to catch up.

They found the old woman staring at a tree stump that looked as if, centuries ago, it had been struck by lightning. "I call this the dial," she said. "What do you see?"

Lizzie took a step closer and looked down onto the stump. Judith had rubbed away some moisture that would soon become frost. The concentric rings of new growth were each, to her newly skilful eyes, differently illuminated. She could feel each colour . . . and somehow flavour . . . leading down into the soil around them, and away under the horizon, where they became . . . associated with the sky. The grammar of the sentences these sensations suggested to her brain, when she tried to put how she felt into words . . . it still amazed her that she could feel and think things language wasn't designed to cope with.

"It's like a network diagram," said Autumn. "Or a nervous system."

"Yes, yes, science," sighed Judith. "Stop reducing it to

it's like this or it's like that. It is the thing it is. Someone, nobody knows who—"

"You mean you don't know," said Autumn.

"—and I'm the last one who might, so that's nobody; someone grew this tree here and tied it carefully to every border that runs in every direction, worldly or otherwise, around the town. The borders were grown into it. Then, I should think as part of that process, it was struck by lightning, as a sacrifice, to give it power of its own, and felled, so everything could be easily seen on the stump. A piece of great magical art, this is. I think when whoever had the trees up here burnt, they might have been trying to get at this."

"Wasn't that Sovo?" Lizzie shuddered at the thought of the company that had set the townsfolk against each other earlier in the year. She still had come nowhere near to matching the money of theirs that she had burned rather than accept.

"I thought so at the time," said Judith. "But I've sniffed the air up here since, and it don't smell like anything else they did."

Lizzie took a tentative sniff and wished she had the same experience of the gifts of the well as Judith had. Everything to do with magic smelled the same to her: like bonfire night when she was eight.

"So what does it tell us?" asked Autumn.

Judith took off her left glove, then the glove underneath that one, and put her bare finger onto the stump. Lizzie flinched as all the colours suddenly flashed into her at once, but a moment later it was obvious that was what Judith had expected to happen. The old lady stood there, lit up like, well, a Christmas tree. Lizzie thought for a moment she had broken into a coughing fit, but then she realised it was Judith's version of laughter. "Oh," she said, "that always tickles my sensibilities. I sometimes come up here when I really don't need to, you know. Come on, you do it, too."

Lizzie looked at Autumn, wondering if this was going to be another moment like when Judith had introduced them to the well water via the distribution mechanism of a bucket. Autumn shrugged, and put her finger beside Judith's, and Lizzie quickly followed suit.

The colours that shot up her arm were definitely . . . welcome in several interesting places. She didn't want to look at Autumn now. Sharing this intimacy was right on the edge of too embarrassing to bear.

"Oh, look at you two, like unicorns at your first orgy," said Judith, for all the world as if that were a thing people said. "Get past that, and if you can't read it with your bits, read it with your brain."

Lizzie did her best to read it with her brain. She could feel a . . . lacking of something, a kind of nausea about something that wasn't working, or that had been . . . interfered with. No, more serious than that, this was like perversion, or . . . she found she was uncomfortable with the concept, but like . . . blasphemy. She tried to see or feel or work out where it was, but couldn't. She looked to Judith, and found that Autumn was doing the same, with a shocked expression.

"I probably got more out of that than you did," said Judith, taking her hand from the stump. "In terms of info, I mean. It turns out that, as I suspected from the fairies getting involved, one of the boundaries has been weakened in an impossible direction."

"You mean in a dimension beyond the four we know about?" said Autumn.

"That's what I said. Which is a bit serious, because when one of those sods steps in, things get all . . ." She did a sudden twisting motion with both hands. "They don't have to pay attention to the boundaries of mind, of memory. The fairies have a lot of trouble with the existence of beings who can do that, because, though they don't like to acknowledge it, they themselves are all about their relationship with human minds and memories, and this lot instead are all . . ." She did the motion again. Lizzie found she really didn't like what it implied. It looked like Judith was turning something inside out. "They can get into your head, mess with what you think you know. It's also harder for us to see the problem. I don't know yet how I can work out exactly what's being done to reality. It feels like it's ongoing, like something that's gathering in strength, echoing back and forth and building up. Still, I think I know a way to see where the initial distortions are."

"So is this anything to do with my ghost?" asked Lizzie.

"If it is," said Judith, "then this might turn out to be a bloody terrifying Christmas."

Lizzie took a few moments to take that in, and realised that if she thought about it at any length . . . no, she needed to keep going. She looked at her watch. "Okay," she said, "very much taken on board, but I've got the wedding couple coming. Give me a call if you find out anything else." The other two agreed that they would, and she headed off down the hill, her boots sliding on the frost that had started to form on the grass. The moon rising behind the hill cast long shadows over her as she made her way back down to the river.

———

Autumn watched Lizzie go, worried for her friend. Lizzie's spirituality sometimes felt like a force field that she used to keep difficult emotional stuff at bay until it all got to be too much. While for Autumn herself, difficult emotional stuff was more of an adventure playground.

She felt Judith's hand land on her arm, like the skeleton grabbing out from one of those old novelty money boxes. "You're with me, my apprentice," she said. "We're going to try summat."

"Every day," said Autumn, "you remind me more of the Emperor from Star Wars."

Judith considered that for a moment. "Nice to finally get a bit of respect," she decided.

Lizzie got back to the Vicarage with ten minutes to spare before the wedding couple were due to arrive, and frantically cleared up her study, which basically involved grabbing everything on the floor and throwing it into a cupboard. She always tried to make the place look welcoming, because wedding couples always arrived with several fallacies in their heads. They thought she was empowered to stop them from getting married, probably after she'd decided they weren't holy enough. But actually, though she herself didn't have to agree to marry them, she had no legal right to stop anyone else doing so, if legally married they could be. They also always thought she was going to talk to them about sex. As if anyone needed "the conversation" these days. As with everything else, they got their ideas of what she did from sitcoms, if anywhere. These were the people who'd decided to take the stress she was always already under and pile on some more.

She heard the sound of a car pulling up in the drive, and went to switch on the kettle. It had boiled before the doorbell rang. Which was right at the moment the kitchen clock indicated was the appointed time. Wow, these two were either very scared or very precise. She opened the door to the very tall Alan Bathurst, and the really quite tiny Emma Beeson, who were both wearing jumpers with Christmas motifs and matching woolly hats and grinning at her like idiots.

"Festive," said Lizzie. "Do come in."

———

"We're going to be a little demanding," said Alan, leaning forward in the sofa in Lizzie's study, and somehow managing to loom from a sitting position. He, like his fiancée, had a rich Swindon accent.

"Oh?" said Lizzie, killing off several sarcastic replies before they could reach her lips.

"Yes," said Emma. "We hope you don't mind. We have made a plan."

Lizzie had been wondering what was in the briefcase

that Alan had placed on the floor in front of them. "An order of service, you mean?"

"Ah, not just that!" Alan beamed as he opened up the case and brought out a series of what looked like professionally designed lists. Lizzie realised with slight horror that this couple had their own logo. "This is what happens before, during, and after, and where everyone and everything should be in the church."

"Do you mind?" said Emma. "It's going to take a bit of doing. But please say it's okay. It's very important to us."

Lizzie leafed slowly through the plans, holding back her every grumpy impulse. "It's . . . not something we'd usually do. What are these 'statues' you've got on the map?"

The couple looked at each other as if it were amazing she'd think there was anything odd about this. "They're from our student halls," said Alan. "You know the stupid stuff most people have in their corridors, traffic cones and all that? Ours went a bit further. We nicked actual—"

"They were nicked at the time," said Emma quickly, "but these statues we've got our eye on are exact replicas, they'd all be bought and paid for."

Lizzie pinched the brow of her nose. She'd never had a wedding couple before who thought she was about to rule out their ability to wed on the basis of multiple counts of robbery. "What sort of statues?"

"You know, the sort you find in . . . now, don't take this the wrong way—" began Alan.

"Churchyards?" finished Lizzie.

Alan pointed at her like she'd got the right answer at charades.

Lizzie wondered exactly what the *right* way to take that would be. But still, there was nothing here that was disallowed. These two weren't attempting to marry at night or to write their own vows, or any of the other things couples couldn't do that sometimes surprised them. She took a moment to calm herself down. "Okay," she said.

"Marvellous," said Alan.

"The order of service looks . . . different. But nothing we can't do. Can you get me the text of these three poems you want people to read?"

She was not at all surprised when Emma immediately slapped paper copies into her hand. She was aware of the couple looking nervously at each other as she read them through. These were probably from some movie she hadn't seen. "All fine," she said, finally.

Emma and Alan visibly relaxed.

———

After she'd shown them out, Lizzie slumped against the door. A sudden wave of exhaustion had washed over her.

Only to be expected. There was only so much protein in a steady diet of tea and cake, and ahead of her was the assault course of multiple Christmas dinners, most of them in public.

She was about to go and put the kettle on for more coffee when she heard the knock at the door.

She wondered for a moment if she'd really heard it. It was a very gentle knock. No, there it was again. There was something odd about it, like it wasn't a person doing it, but a branch somehow tapping against the front door.

Lizzie eased herself into a standing position. The knock came again. It had grown neither more insistent nor less. That was what had made her think of nature, rather than a person. If it were someone, why didn't they ring the doorbell?

Why was she hesitating to just have a look? This was probably an elderly parishioner, out in the cold and possibly needing her help. Chiding herself, she opened the door.

The little boy stood on her doorstep, the night behind him, the lights of the park opposite shining through him. He was looking at her. His expression was desperately in need of something.

Lizzie was afraid of him, and at the same time guilty for being afraid of him. That sense of culpability made her feel like the victim in a horror story, that she deserved whatever he'd come to do. But what was he here to do?

She wanted to slam the door closed on him. The fear was making her want to do that. Everything she stood for, though, stood against giving in to that fear. She knew, somehow, that to do that would doom her. She suddenly felt like she was on the edge of a cliff. But what did that feeling mean?

She took a deep breath, made herself calm, and squatted down to the boy's level. "You can come in if you want," she said.

The little boy looked perhaps slightly less lost, just for a moment.

Then he vanished, without Lizzie ever quite seeing the moment he'd done so, and she found she was looking only at the lights and the dark and the drizzle.

There was a sudden sound from behind her. It was a sound she hadn't heard before. But it had only been the house settling, right? Just one of the many noises this place made, most of which she'd gotten used to.

She closed the door and tried to go back to work, but couldn't.

She went to search the Vicarage, switching on lights wherever she went. She didn't find anything, except a series of sounds that always seemed to be just in the next room, that she could never find the source of.

She couldn't help dwelling on what she'd just done, on

the risk—given what she now knew about the world and what was threatening it—that she had taken.

She had invited the ghost inside.

2

Autumn had half expected Judith to lead her back to her own home, but it turned out this was yet another occasion on which the older woman was not going to let her over her threshold. Autumn and Lizzie had never, in fact, been to Judith's house. Instead, Autumn realised Judith was heading for the Plough, which was, frankly, fine by her.

The interior of the little pub had been decorated by the landlord, Rob, with his customary largesse. A small Christmas tree sat in the corner, there were three streamers on the roof beams, and, noted Autumn with a slight twinge of worry, a hopeful sprig of what looked like real mistletoe was hanging right in the middle of the ceiling of the front bar, by the log burner. "Biberomancy," said Judith, taking a seat at the bar, and ignoring a couple of worried looks from the locals.

"Divination by ... drink?" Autumn felt a little awkward to so obviously be here with Judith. Being the owner of a magic shop had given her a rather jolly and sociable relationship with the townsfolk. She was the local eccentric from a local family, who didn't mind a bit of laughter at her expense. She'd gone along with that wholeheartedly. It was either that or . . . well, end up like Judith.

"By beer, or at least that's how I use the word."

Rob, looking wary, all seven feet of him, with a beard about as long, had taken his place behind the bar facing Judith. "Don't see much of you in here, Mrs. Mawson. What'll it be?"

"A pint of your worst."

Rob's beard visibly bristled. "I do not keep a bad ale. They're all Arkells, mind, which some people don't like, but them's that don't don't come in here. Shall I just pick one at random?"

"Two pints of 3B," Autumn said quickly.

"That'll do," said Judith.

Rob considered for a moment, then nodded to Autumn. "Because it's you, Miss Witchcraft." He started to pull the beers.

"Why," whispered Autumn, "did you have to say that?"

"Because now the beers will be given to us with emotional content," said Judith.

"Did it have to be *negative* emotional content?"

Judith glared at her. "How many times does the world have to show you, you don't get summat for nothing?"

Under Rob's wary gaze, they took their beers into the

front bar to sit by the log burner. "So what do we do?"

"We get rat-arsed—" said Judith.

"We both have work tomorrow—"

"—while repeating certain phrases and gestures, and these phrases and gestures will be distorted by the inebriation in a way which directly indicates the shape the town is being bent into. So I'll be able to see where the distortions are."

Autumn liked a pint or two around Christmas time. However, she couldn't help thinking that Judith wouldn't be much of a drinking companion. "Is it okay if we chat to people we know?"

Judith paused for a moment so long that Autumn thought she'd offended her, but no, of course that wasn't possible. "As long as you keep up the incantation every ten minutes. Follow me." She started to make a series of sounds in the back of her throat, and Autumn, grateful for the Christmas hits playing over the speakers, began to attempt to copy her.

———————

In order to fully participate in her social evening, therefore, Autumn found herself greeting the many friends who entered, getting up to stand with them in the main bar, then retreating quickly every ten minutes to huddle with Judith, claiming either that she was cold or having a coughing fit.

"Are you directing your germs at her?" asked Mick, the car mechanic. "Is this biological warfare?"

"She's working at the shop now," said Autumn. "It'd be rude not to bring her along."

"Keeps her off the streets, I suppose," said Paul the builder. "Now she can just be rude in the one place."

Other residents chimed in with similar comments, and, after a few token protests of hers turned the tide a bit—because in the end, these were kind and polite people—Autumn changed the subject. She hadn't really grasped until this evening just how disliked Judith was in Lychford. When she returned to the log burner, the old woman was looking into the fire, her face a mask. Surely, over the years, that background dislike must seep into you, must change you? Was that what Autumn was going to end up like? *Alone,* part of her said, but Judith wasn't actually alone, was she? Autumn couldn't remember, quite, what the details were, and now she thought about it, she was sure she'd once heard someone in town refer to Judith as a widow, but she was equally certain Judith had made reference to someone waiting for her at home. "How's your husband?" she asked.

"Piss off," said Judith. Then immediately followed it with the required noises, meaning Autumn had to join in.

Autumn had now had three pints. Being told it was imperative that one should drink had an effect. Like one of those social experiment . . . things. It did mean, however, that she wasn't going to take that on the nose, and when she'd completed the noises she said so. "You coming out with stuff like that is why that lot don't like you. What's wrong with me asking about your husband?"

"You're not really asking. You're just making conversation."

Autumn was about to reply with her usual compassion when the door of the pub opened. In walked a young man, built, as was obvious even through his hefty pullover and coat, like a rugby player. He had one of those beards that all the blokes had started getting a couple of years back, but it looked . . . all right. Tended to. His eyes were bright and interesting, and he had the most enormous grin on his face. Calls from local lads suggested he was known around here. "Good evening," he said in return, and his voice was exactly the right sort of posh, immediately suggesting he was somehow laughing at himself.

He was . . . yeah, on a second and a third viewing, he really was very damn attractive.

"Yeah," said Autumn to Judith, "you're right. Sorry. I'd better get on with the drinking. Same again?" She was up and heading for the mutual acquaintances before Judith could utter another syllable.

———————

It turned out the new arrival was called Luke, and he was a tutor at the agricultural college who'd also been working on one of the local farms with Ben and Kerry Rosset, the locals who'd greeted him with such bonhomie. Autumn immediately offered to get a round in, and Luke, with just a glance to the Rossets to confirm this wasn't some drunken loony, agreed. This many pints down, and aware she'd only have ten minutes before having to withdraw, Autumn felt she had to talk fast. Perhaps a bit too fast. She immediately told him all about her shop, and Ed, who kept the tropical fish at the garden centre, wandered over and added the quaint detail that she was friends with the local vicar and employed the local crank. That one, over there. Luke actually waved.

Judith seemed to consider for a moment, then experimentally raised a hand in response. It looked after a moment like she'd felt something on the surface of her palm, and turned it to examine it.

"She seems . . . weird," said Luke.

"She really is," said Autumn, who'd taken the opportunity of him turning around to check his finger for a wedding ring. There was none. She'd already given him several opportunities to use the word girlfriend, and he'd seized none of them. "So the agricultural college, they have a wild social life, we hear a lot of stories. . . ." Which got a laugh from the Rossets.

"It's all true. Not that I can partake. At the end of the evening I head sadly home to my lonely staff apartment."

Was it her imagination, or was he checking her out, too? Right, she needed to come out with something that would indicate she was on a whole different level to any farming women he might know. Something that would say she was not only matey, but full of witchy wisdom, the cunning woman of the shadows. "So," she said, "are you watching *Strictly Come Dancing*?"

A blur of conversation gradually got lost somewhere in darkness, and there was probably some . . . kissing . . . and then she must have fallen asleep because where was she now, exactly? Oh. *Phew.* At home in bed. All the familiar details of that cupboard over there; hello, cupboard. Oh . . . she felt . . . she felt . . . no, managed to keep that down. Still a bit drunk, too, so this was going to hurt even more later. Still, it was Christmas. She'd just gotten a bit too festive. But there'd been something important. Oh, right, Judith. Their magical mission. Well, she'd done

her bit. Probably. She remembered Judith had said something to her, late on, had tried to get through to her
about . . . right, well, maybe she herself hadn't learned
anything, but she hoped Judith had.

Okay, time to slowly get moving, find out where her
feet were, get some serious coffee into . . .

She felt something move in bed beside her.

She looked across and saw the naked back of a man.
Whose name was . . . no, that wasn't coming to her. And
it was also now suddenly very important that she was
naked, too.

Oh no. *Oh* no.

"Oh, hi, are you awake?" He turned over and looked
anxiously at her. At least he didn't look like the cat who'd
gotten the cream. *Had* he gotten the cream? It didn't
quite . . . feel like he had. She realised she hadn't said anything, and was just looking at him in a way which was
getting a very worried reaction. "Nothing happened," he
said quickly. "Please don't worry."

"We're naked!"

"You kind of . . . insisted on that. I tried to get out
of bed a couple of times, but you'd switched the light
off, and I couldn't see anything, and I couldn't find my
clothes, and it was cold—"

"How do I know you're telling the truth?"

He suddenly looked very serious. "Because I would

never—you *wanted* to, but you were about to pass out."

She wished her new senses could tell her if someone was lying. But no, she didn't need that. Just by looking at him, she could see he was offended by the mere implication, and worried for her, too. She nodded. "Okay."

"Okay. So. Would you like to . . . talk about it?"

"What?"

"This." He gestured vaguely at them both. At least she hoped that's what he was gesturing at.

She could only shake her head.

"Well . . . that leaves us with the option of one of us closing our eyes while the other finds clothes, and us never speaking of this again."

Autumn was about to agree when her mobile, on the bedside table, rang. Gathering the covers to her in a way which suddenly made her feel like she was in an American TV show, she saw who it was, hesitated, then felt she had to answer it.

"Quickly," said Judith's voice on the other end of the line. "What's going on there?" She sounded urgent. The volume on the phone was loud enough that the guy . . . whose name still escaped her . . . could hear every word.

"Nothing. Why do you ask?"

"I mean, is anything unusual happening to you?"

Autumn wanted to say really, yes, there was. But she knew this wasn't the sort of unusual Judith meant. "No."

"That young man who's there with you, is there anything strange about him?"

Autumn was about to say, yes, he seemed weirdly decent, when she felt a sudden movement beside her, and turned to see more than she should have seen, as the guy . . . whose name would come to her soon . . . was getting quickly out of bed and grabbing for his clothes. "I should be off," he said. "Sorry." He gestured at the phone. "Interestingly intimate relationship you two . . . anyway, early start. Sorry again. Really sorry."

"No, wait—"

But he was off, out of the door and down the stairs, looking back to awkwardly wave, then clearly feeling he was in the wrong and shouldn't be chancing a merry gesture. A moment later Autumn heard the shop door close. Which meant she'd left it unlocked last night.

"Well?" said Judith on the phone. "He's gone now, so you can tell me."

"That's all you're bloody getting," said Autumn, reflecting that that might as well be the title of her autobiography. "Apart from he wasn't strange at all, he was . . . great. And I'm fine. So you needn't worry." As Judith started to say something equally urgent, Autumn switched off the phone and threw it after—

Luke. That had been his name.

She heard the phone bounce down the stairs and then

the sound of glass shattering. Then something dripping.

Autumn threw the covers back over her head and waited for death.

———————

Judith tried a couple of times to call Autumn, but the phone kept going to voicemail. She would have to go over there.

In the pub, Judith had made a series of notes on a beer mat, comparing how far Autumn's magical shouts differed from what they should have been, and had thankfully gotten everything she'd needed before Autumn had abandoned the magical working altogether, snogged that lad's face off and dragged him out of the pub to, as she'd put it, "show him her wise and shadowy artefacts." The sampling she'd taken on her palm had told her something was wrong, but it had also told her it was going to take time to work out what it was.

That morning, before it was light, Judith had taken her notes and compared them to those she'd taken that summer, on a particularly placid day when she'd decided Lychford was about as normal as it was ever going to get.

That had given her a musical sense of the nature of the distortions. At dawn, ignoring what younger, weaker women would call a hangover, she'd climbed to a high place overlooking the town, and come out with a shout that approximated the gap between how things should be and where they were now. The resonances of that shout returned, to her enhanced senses, an idea of where the distortions were. As she'd suspected, they weren't fixed, but building, like water slapping back and forth as the ground underneath it juddered in a gathering earthquake.

It was where those distortions were focussed that worried her most: at the magic shop; at the Vicarage; at Judith's own home. With Lizzie and Autumn in their beds, that might mean they themselves, or, in Autumn's case, who they were with, had been got at. In Judith's own case . . . she had a horrible feeling she'd already felt the change in her own home without registering it as important. It had happened to someone . . . something . . . that was such a regular part of her life that she tended to overlook . . . him.

She would have to tell Lizzie and Autumn about this as soon as possible, but first she had to deal with her own house. Judith went to the foot of the stairs and looked up them, bracing herself. She could feel the coldness from down here, had gotten used to sleeping beside it, even. She knew she deserved this curse, for employing the darkest of workings, decades ago. But she couldn't say she'd changed. As soon as summat difficult had blocked her path, when the three of them had come together to resist Sovo, she had gone straight back to the darkness.

She put one foot on the bottom step. Arthur's voice, of course, immediately came from upstairs. "You been out already, woman! You been off with your fancy man?"

"Course I have," she called back. "We've been making mad passionate love in the dewy grass. You hang on, I'll tell you all about it." She'd been doing the minimum for Arthur in the last few days, just nodding in the direction of her duty of care. Taking care of him was a nonsense, she knew it was, but she couldn't seem to help it. Perhaps that was part of the curse. Or maybe it was just human nature. If it was, that said good things about her which she wasn't quite willing to believe. She started to climb the stairs.

"You don't even want to see me during the day. You spend all your time with that whore now. Encouraging her. Letting what she does get your juices flowing."

"Summat has to, because you can't!" Judith's mind was racing. Had that been a reference to what Autumn had got up to last night? If so, how did Arthur know about that? It wasn't as if she shared information with him.

Judith had to pause for her usual moment on the threshold before going into her bedroom and finding Arthur, or rather what she had to start making herself think of as the ghost of him, attached to his ventilator, which was, unlike him, entirely real and a burden to her electricity bill. He was, as always, watching his whodunits on Sky, the remote, which was also a real artefact, accessible to his fingertips whenever he wanted them to be solid. He met her gaze with his usual baleful expression. "Oh, you've decided to come and spend a few moments with me. I'm honoured."

"You should be." If whatever distortion of reality had touched Lizzie and Autumn had also reached out in her direction via what might well look to it like her weak point, via Arthur, then it might have also made itself vulnerable. If it had altered him, then perhaps she could learn something here. She had to make use of Arthur to seize that thing which was trying to sneak up on them all, and was building and building towards something terrible.

She made herself sit down on the side of the bed next to his chair. She watched *Murder, She Wrote* for a few moments. Some people were being very jolly about a corpse. She tried not to think about what she was contemplating. She kept her eyes fixed on the screen and slowly made herself reach out. Her fingers touched the ice of Arthur's head. There was a sense memory there, a little charade of familiar skin. That softness where he hadn't shaved for about four days. The scent of him came to her, so familiar in this place as to be normally unnoticed, but back at the centre of her senses now, the same as when they'd met. With it, the memory of dances in the town hall. That suit he'd worn with chalk on the cuffs, his lapels always so scuffed. She made the hand go further, through the skin, something she'd never before dared do. Why would she have? She'd known when she'd first seen him here that he was a punishment that had been entirely deserved. She'd never tried to escape him. Though she also longed to. Stupid.

"What you doing, woman?" He said it with the same playful tone as when she used to reach out for him in bed. He knew how to play every note of her. He was her curse. With every inch her hand reached, she felt more and more like she was compromising herself with intimacy, holding desperately to a corpse, a corpse that had infected her, had hurt her, and why, oh why, had she been so weak, so foolish, to never tell anyone? She was like her friends who didn't go to the doctor and had died out of pride. Only this had lasted much longer. She was sobbing, she realised. He was chuckling at the sound.

Her hand reached a point of nothingness, right inside Arthur. She flexed her fingers in the darkness at the centre of what had started as his body, but was now pure void. It really should have come out the other side, but there was more space inside him than looked possible on the outside. "Judith?" he said suddenly, and his voice now was horribly different now. "Judith, is that you?"

"Of course it's me!" she managed to blurt out.

"I don't know where I am. I'm inside something. I can't see you. Give me your hand!" The words were still being spoken by the cold ghost sitting next to her, but they sounded distant, echoing from the impossible space inside him, and different, loving, young. Was *her* Arthur really somewhere inside this thing? How had she not realised that? Or had she always known it? Was this the change the ripple across reality from the border had made?

She was stretching out her fingers before she could even frame the thought. She was trying to reach the real Arthur.

Something brushed the tips of her fingers. A hand that was about to close on hers.

Its fingertips were cold.

She jerked away. The hand grabbed hers. She yelled, and tried to wrench out of its grasp. It had locked onto her hand. She looked urgently at Arthur, and he was grinning all over his face, which lapped like a pool of water around her arm, his features distorted by her being inside him, and he said, with that bitter, clever voice back in place again, "One down, two to go."

It was a trap, she realised, one that had been baited with love and with her own arrogance.

Judith had no time to cry out before the hand inside Arthur, impossibly strong, heaved on hers, and she fell headlong into her husband.

———————

Over the next few days, Lizzie attended another Christmas dinner, this one at Deanery Chapter, with a lot of other local vicars all looking equally put upon, and the conversation deliberately bright and cheerful to the point of mutual hysteria. She couldn't help feeling the others were only under the normal pressures of Christmas, and didn't have to deal with whatever was weighing down on her. Then she presided over a carol service at the school, after which a mother had told her that those carols had been much better than the ones in church, not so religious.

Most nights now she was working late, trying to put out of her mind the little noises from elsewhere in the Vicarage. She was hardly sleeping. The stress seemed to be increasing every day. It was like she was missing something that was heading straight for her. Her plans for re-organising the crib service in order to bring a few more actual children into it weren't getting very far. So when she saw the familiar number on her phone, Lizzie was more than ready to give in to the distraction. Besides, she'd probably reached capacity on her answer phone. She hadn't spoken to Autumn in days, not since the tree stump. She had been unconsciously waiting, she realised, for Judith to call them all together and explain what this subtle threat they were facing was all about. She'd been ignoring the possibility that the answer might involve her. "Hey, how are you?"

The voice at the other end of the line had an undercurrent of desperation to it that it took a moment for Lizzie to realise she actually felt nostalgic about. This was Autumn as a student all over again. "Kind of . . . weird . . ." And she went on to describe her night at the Plough and the morning after and how awkward she'd felt in the days since.

"So," said Lizzie, when she could get a word in edgewise, "what did you and this guy Luke actually end up, you know, doing?"

"I may have . . . jingled his bells."

"But did you jingle all the way?"

"I don't think so, and you're smiling at having come up with that line, aren't you?"

Lizzie deliberately killed her grin. "Do we have to hunt him down and . . . actually, no, don't tell Judith about this, she really would want to hunt him down."

"I don't think he did anything wrong, I think he was kind of . . . lovely, actually, and Judith already tried to sort of warn me about him. She hasn't been in to work since, or I'd have asked her what that was about. I haven't gone after her because I kind of want to sack her, but then she might sack me, or worse, not, and then she'd be completely in charge of me."

"Did you get Luke's number?"

"I . . . found it. About lunchtime that same day. When I went for a shower. I don't know why I wanted him to write it down there. I copied it using a mirror."

"You know you're wonderful, don't you?"

"You're smiling again, at my distress."

"Are you going to call him?"

There was a long pause. "I've already called him—"

"Not at all needy."

"—eight times—"

"Indeed, 'needy' is absolutely not a word I would use."

"—and left eight voicemail messages."

"Saying what? Needily."

"That I want to apologise to him, to try to explain—"

"You once told me you always did what the Duke of Wellington said, 'never explain, never apologise'—"

"Yeah, and you told me the Duke of Wellington ended up as the most hated man in Britain. And I don't want to be like that. I don't want to keep working through a list of rom-com clichés. But I don't want to be alone, okay? And I'm fed up with . . . trying without it looking like I'm trying. He was lovely, and I've fucked it up. Like I always fuck everything up . . . I'm sorry."

"Come on over."

"No, it's fine, I just . . . I love him."

"What?"

There was silence for a moment. "I shouldn't have said that. I'm messed up. I'm going to try to get some sleep."

"Autumn, wait—" But she'd hung up. Lizzie immediately tried to dial her back, but the call went straight to voicemail. She thought about going over, but it was late. There had been an edge of weird desperation to her friend's voice that Lizzie hadn't heard before. Sleep might be the best thing for her. Like it would be for her.

"No hurting," said the small voice from the doorway.

Lizzie looked up to see the little boy again, and yet again the sight chilled her. He had both his hands up as if to hopelessly defend himself. "No hurting," he repeated, imploring.

"Are you . . . afraid of *me*?" asked Lizzie, getting slowly to her feet. If so, why had he come into her house? The movement seemed to startle the boy. He turned and vanished even as Lizzie took a step forward. She stopped, and rubbed her brow. "Coffee," she said. "Maybe some rum."

———

Autumn lay in her bed and tried to sleep. She had never felt like this before. She felt weirdly guilty at having let Lizzie hear a little of it. The feeling had risen up in her during the afternoon, and made her keep going back to her phone, keep trying Luke's number, over and over, until with an effort of will she'd called Lizzie instead. She was breathing harder than she normally would, a great weight of twitching anxiety in her chest. She wanted to hear Luke's voice, to have him reassure her that she hadn't offended him, that everything was okay, that she would see him again. That might lead to more. No, that wasn't the most important thing, just being okay with him, that was where it had to start.

The same set of thoughts rolled over and over in her head. She should make herself get undressed, have a hot drink. How was she ever going to sleep? She clutched the covers in order to feel something in her hands. She'd been in love, possibly, a couple of times in her life. She thought that was probably what people would call the sensation she'd felt on those other occasions: a nervousness about the bloke in question finding someone else, a desire to make sure everything was okay between them. But this was ten, twenty times as intense. She'd made herself think that he might have someone else, and she'd been suddenly filled with hatred towards an imaginary person, the agricultural-student nature of whom she'd sketched out in her mind to the point where her rival had a ponytail and a checked shirt. Like someone in a musical.

She was going to be alone at Christmas, when a tally was made of who was alone and who wasn't and loneliness became a thing everyone talked about. She was going to be alone and in love. Was this what love was going to be like for her from now on? This was so not her.

Autumn closed her eyes and tried to will herself to sleep.

———————

Days are not days as we know them in the places where Finn, Prince of the Blood, walked and thought, far from the fields we know, and whether these were places and whether or not that was walking or thinking, these are also not exactly what we'd mean by those words.

But let's say there was a moment when he came to the edge of Lychford, and he was thinking of why—since he'd been so urgent last time, since his message had been one of impending danger—he'd heard nothing since from the three whose mission it was to protect the borders of this place.

He moved, proudly and unhesitatingly, to cross those borders himself, intending to manifest once more to Autumn and ask what progress had been made.

He stepped not through, but straight past.

Shocked, he tried again. Again, the border to step over eluded him.

Scared and furious now, he bellowed and struck where the border should be, bringing something like lightning and sunlight and gravity together all at once where his fist hit—

—nothing.

He stared at the gap in the realities. This wasn't possible. The worlds had been rearranged, entirely without the permission of his people or anyone else, to cut off the humans inside from all aid.

Finn calmed himself, then turned and said a word and ran, became a light and a hare that skipped over hills and was the wind and was the hills and would get to where his people existed at the speed of the word leaving his mouth. His father had to know of this. He had not the faintest idea what even his people might do to stop this. The worlds had been turned inside out. There might already be horrors abroad in Lychford.

With four days to go before Christmas, Lizzie got to the church early and had everything ready for the wedding rehearsal before Alan and Emma and their families and supporters arrived. At least this was something she'd gotten down to a fine art. This lot, of course, had all their added extras. Indeed, they'd brought along a couple of examples of the statues they were going to place in the church on the day.

"So why do you want . . . this, exactly?" she said, looking up at a carved face that was veined, bulbous, not really much of a face at all. The body of the thing was also not something you'd expect to stand in a churchyard without comment. Those were wings, weren't they? Sort of. Too many arms, really. The whole thing looked like a melted cherub.

"Sentimental reasons," Alan said with a laugh.

"This is exactly like the first one we, *err*, pinched, when we were students," said Emma. Her maids of honour nodded, like this was a story they'd heard often. They were an interesting pair themselves, identical, but Lizzie had been assured they weren't twins. They had eyes that were strikingly green and sort of golden at the same time. Alan's best man, Derek, was also quite something. He must have been over eight feet tall, and Lizzie hadn't really gotten a good look at him, because his face was somehow continually hidden in shadow. He was now carrying the second statue, just as ugly as the first, to the specific spot where this lot wanted it placed.

The father of the bride, Stewart, was present only as a shaft of pulsing green light, which seemed to emanate from somewhere under the floor and faded into the roof. Lizzie had been assured he was going to wear something more formal for the ceremony itself. She leafed back through her forms, worried that she was somehow missing something. But no, there didn't seem to be anything odd going on. "Where did you say you were from?" She should know that, shouldn't she? She should know that offhandedly.

"Swindon," said Emma. "So not too far to drive."

"Are we okay with the order of service now?" asked Alan.

Lizzie wanted to say that actually this was the first thought she'd had about it since the night she'd last seen them, but no, bright and professional, that was the way. She'd had no notes last time she'd read through it, eccentric as it was. She could hardly remember anything about it. She took it from her papers and noticed there was one point she should ask about. "What do you have for the moment when I have to—?"

Emma, of course, had produced a doll of a baby before she'd finished the sentence.

"And here's the other thing," said Alan, putting a very heavy ceremonial knife into her hands. "I'm assuming you won't have one of your own."

Everyone laughed. Lizzie took the doll and the knife up to the font. "And it should be up here, at the end of the service?"

"Right at the climax," said Emma.

"But on the day itself—?" Lizzie couldn't help feeling, as she stood there, the point of the knife sticking into the plastic of the doll, that she was missing something rather important. Was there a point of procedure about this that she hadn't got straight? Why was something inside her screaming that she shouldn't be doing it? She sighed inwardly. Her brain was such a jumble at the moment. Bloody Christmas.

"Don't worry," Alan assured her, "on the day itself, we've already arranged to get hold of the real thing."

———

Autumn tried to work. She went downstairs each morning, made herself get as far as the door, attempted to swing the sign on it from CLOSED to OPEN . . . but if it wasn't to do with getting Luke into her life, what was the point? She was barely sleeping, just finally giving in to exhaustion in the early hours.

One evening, she went over to the Vicarage, hoping to find Lizzie, who was now not answering her phone any more than Luke was. She was surprised to find the Lizzie who opened the door was looking as pale and nervous as she did. "It's not going to snow," she said, without even a hello. "No white Christmas this year."

"Can I come in?"

Lizzie gestured impatiently that she could and Autumn entered, startled about what she'd just noticed about Lizzie's hands. But no, never mind that, that wasn't important, she had something urgent to ask. "So, have you heard from Luke?"

"Who?"

Autumn held in the sudden fury she felt at that impudent question. "Luke! My Luke!"

"Is that the bloke you—? I've never met him. Why should I have heard from him?" Sounding very distracted, Lizzie led her into the kitchen, where . . . oh my God.

A small boy stood in the middle of the room, weeping. On seeing Lizzie, he instantly grabbed for her hand. "No hurting!" he shouted.

Lizzie sighingly pulled her cardigan sleeve away from him and pushed past him to get to the kettle. This, Autumn realised, must be that ghost Lizzie had told them about. Back when . . . yeah, Judith hadn't been into the shop for ages now, what was that about? But no, there were more urgent matters at hand. "I think there were some specific words I said to Luke that he didn't like, or maybe it was the way I said them. Should I go over to the agricultural college, do you think?"

Lizzie made a sudden gasp of pain that made Autumn look over to where she was washing out two cups. She'd gotten the water on her hands, and the backs of her hands were ...

"Sorry," said Lizzie. "For some reason I've been trying to stop myself from being able to use my hands. It's the stupidest thing. I can only hurt them for a little while before I can't manage it anymore. I've tried burning them with candles, sticking them with a screwdriver. I can't quite bring myself to use the scissors but, you know, I'm going to have to get to that soon, or it'll be, I don't know, too late."

"No hurting!" yelled the boy.

Autumn was stunned for a moment by the horror her friend was inflicting upon herself. But hey, it was nothing compared to what she was going through. "You think you've got problems? I think I've now filled up Luke's voicemail. Or he's switched it off—"

"Will you just stop—!" That had been a sudden shout from Lizzie. The kettle was now starting to boil. "Sorry, sorry, I need to concentrate. Making you tea just gave me an idea. I should have seen it sooner. I'm going to try boiling water on my hands. See if I can ruin them completely."

"Why . . . why—?"

"Then I'll be useless to them. I won't be able to do the thing." She made a stabbing motion. "I've tried everything else. I don't know who this 'I' is I'm talking about. Myself, I'm fine. Just a bit busy. There's just . . . you know, something inside, trying to do something to stop all this."

"All what? If you can't listen to this important stuff I'm telling you about Luke for five minutes—"

"No hurting!"

"That can wait. This is important." The kettle was boiling furiously. Lizzie snatched it off its stand and made to pour the water over her hand.

Reflexively, Autumn leapt forward and knocked the kettle into the sink.

Lizzie cried out, pushed Autumn away, and grabbed for the kettle. Autumn, furious at her, tried to get it off her.

"Don't!" cried the little boy.

Lizzie slapped Autumn as hard as she had ever been hit by anyone.

Autumn fell to the floor, clutching her face.

"Oh no, oh no," whispered Lizzie. Then she took the kettle again and started to refill it.

Autumn was panting, feeling the anger, the adrenalin . . . breaking down something inside her. She wanted to hurt Lizzie back for this, more than anything, so she could get back to . . . get back to . . .

Oh no. Oh no, what was happening here?

She heaved herself up and grabbed Lizzie's wrists, making her drop the kettle. "Do that again."

Without hesitation, Lizzie broke free and did so.

Autumn yelled with the impact, but this time she was ready for it. This time she could feel clearly the sudden insight it brought. She grabbed her friend, and started to heave her towards the door, Lizzie fighting all the way. "Okay, you . . . you keep doing that. You keep slapping me. But you're coming with me."

"No! I'm busy! I have to hurt my hands!"

"No hurting!" the child cried desperately, turning to watch them go.

"Listen to him," said Autumn, hoping against hope she could keep this anger going. "This isn't normal. We've been got at."

———————

Lizzie kept flexing her fingers in her gloves as her friend drove through the rain-lashed darkness. This was a complete waste of time, when she had so much to do, and her hands were still functional, and that was breaking her heart.

"It's good," said a small voice from the backseat.

Lizzie looked over her shoulder to see that bloody boy still sitting there, shivering. She was furious that he'd followed her. Only . . . she somehow felt that she'd wanted him to as well. She was doing her best, she was doing all she could do, while part of her, a stupid part, kept trying to hurt her hands . . . or was it the other way around?

"Hit me again," said Autumn. "I'm starting to . . . to go where we're going for a different reason."

"You're driving, and I'm wearing mittens, you stupid—!"

Autumn made a desperate sound, then reached over to the stereo in the battered old Ford Fiesta and shoved in the CD that had been sticking out of the player. The sound of Greg Lake erupted into the car.

Lizzie made a sound of her own and hit Autumn again.

Autumn swung the car down the driveway and past the sign saying "Hartford Lodge Agricultural College," and as she did so she began desperately to sing along.

———————

Luke Halsall was looking forward to going home. Tonight he'd gone for a Christmas pint with his students, then he had some paperwork to do, and he'd be off before lunchtime tomorrow, down south, back to his friends. The nature of his job meant he couldn't keep his phone switched off, but he'd managed to assign that Autumn woman a different ringtone, a warning siren, and took care to let it go to voicemail whenever she called. He'd been going to call her back after the first message, but before he could, she'd left loads of them, and his guilt had turned into annoyance, then worry. That night had been such a mistake. He'd kept going over it in his head, but no, he thought he'd done the right thing. It seemed like the owner of the magic shop was the villain of one of those horror stories where one *didn't* have to do something wrong in order to have someone go the full bunny boiler on you.

Which was a huge pity, because he'd really liked her. When she'd been drunk in the pub she'd been good fun. Apart from her having to keep popping back to the corner to keep that nosy old woman company while she practiced her folk songs. That had maybe been a bit of a warning sign. Even the next morning, she'd acted in an entirely understandable way, but then . . . that phone call by, again, that old woman . . .

His thoughts had kept Luke, as he walked back across the darkened campus towards the tutors' quarters, from looking at what was ahead of him. But now, as he neared the corner of his housing block, he wondered what the odd shape was he was seeing there by his door. Was someone waiting in the shadows? Oh no, it wasn't—?!

Autumn stepped out to confront him. "It's okay," she said. "I'm not going to try to force you into anything." Another figure stepped out beside her. Autumn looked between them, as if only now realising what this looked like. "That's absolutely not why I brought along a vicar."

———————————

Against his better judgment, Luke let them into his flat. The presence of another person in his slightly personalised abode of vinyl record player and specialist coffee maker, even one as weirdly tense as this vicar seemed, made him feel slightly safer. This was surely that friend of Autumn's that people had talked about. Maybe this would be a chance to put an end to this. "Listen—" he began.

"I'm not weird," said Autumn, interrupting him. "At least, not so long as she keeps on—Lizzie—?" The vicar slapped Autumn around the face. "Thanks. Now—"

Luke took a step back. What the hell? "Okay, I've changed my mind, I think you should go—"

"Please, just listen to me, just for a few minutes. That's all I ask."

"Okay." He waited.

He realised she was looking at him with a kind of giddy joy, that she'd drifted off, but this time she stopped herself before the vicar could move in to slap her. "I understand, in my moments of clarity, that I've been pursuing you in a scary, intense way. I think . . ." She seemed to choose her words carefully. "Something's upset my brain chemistry." The vicar picked up a stapler and started to play with it. Autumn grabbed it off her. "This isn't the usual me. I was hoping that if I came to see you, you might be able to talk me down, but with how I'm feeling now I'm here, nope, not going to happen. So now I need your help in a different way."

She seemed to know what she was talking about. It was quite a relief to hear that voice he'd heard that first night. Luke had had an uncle who'd been schizophrenic, and this understanding of her own condition reminded him of how he'd been sometimes. He carefully sat down and faced her. "What can I do?"

Autumn took something from her bag. "Look at this."

She handed it to him and he found he was looking at a saucer full of some sort of potpourri, which he couldn't help taking a sniff of, and it smelled really weird, kind of—

He managed only a croak as darkness welled up into his head.

———

Autumn looked down at Luke's body where it had fallen onto the sofa. He started to snore. "Okay," she said, "help me . . ." She wanted to ask for Lizzie's help undressing him, but that took her back to the awful reason she'd put the sleep powders into her bag in the first place. "Roll up his sleeve. And keep slapping me. Lizzie, stay with me!"

Lizzie had a jam jar in her hands, and had been about to smash it, Autumn had realised. Now she quickly nodded, distracted beyond distraction, holding on to the same tiny thread of helping each other that was keeping Autumn herself going. The little ghost that had accompanied them here looked anxiously at them. Lizzie squatted down and administered the required slap to Autumn, which she was starting to find bracing, then the two of them got to work on Luke's shirt. Autumn found the syringe in her bag, part of the alchemical kit she always carried, fitted a new needle, and drew out . . . well, who knew how much blood was going to be enough? She was making up this recipe based on nothing more than instinct and what little Judith had managed to teach her. Oh, Judith. She'd been deliberately kept distracted from thinking about Judith. "We have to look for Judith," she said. "She must have been got at, too. But first we have to get back to the shop." She put the syringe full of blood back in her bag, and made Luke as comfortable as she could. She looked down at him on the sofa, tousled, lost. He'd been ready to listen to her, even at this extremity. "Keep slapping me," she said to Lizzie. "Slap me lots."

Autumn was well aware that the rules for "love potions" were very strict. This was one of those areas where one could easily wander off the path into curse magic and thus invite horrors into one's own life. All love potions could do, she'd told several young customers, was help make someone's mind up about what they really wanted. They couldn't influence that decision, not without terrible penalties. However, Autumn was aware that there were recipes for potions that claimed to be able to do just that. So what if you took such a recipe, but picked every opposite ingredient, and added, as always in these cases, something associated with the target of one's affections, and blood was the biggest association of all . . .

"What's the opposite of vanilla?" she asked Lizzie, as they stood in the back-room laboratory area of the shop, water already bubbling in the cauldron. Autumn had taken the precaution of wrapping the Reverend's hands in three layers of gloves, held on with elastic bands, so at least she'd have some warning if she was going to try any more self-harm. The inability to use her hands seemed, fortunately, to have satisfied her, and she was staring into space, the conflict inside her playing out only in the tiniest of tics. Beside her stood the ghost child, looking desperately between them.

Lizzie shook her head, snapped back to reality by the question. "Kinky?"

Just the sound of it made Autumn sad. It was like Lizzie's sense of humour had forced its way up out of her, but the face it came from hadn't noticed. "Tuttifrutti," she decided, and got some ice cream from the fridge to provide the first ingredient. Her own brain kept rolling around with the idea of whether Luke would like the smell of vanilla, and shouldn't she go back and see how he was, and of course the slaps were going to be a bit muffled now, so she'd better bloody get on with it. She rushed around the lab, grabbing what she could, letting her unconscious guide her. "The opposite of rose is . . . thorn! The opposite of sugar is . . . salt. The opposite of lemon is . . . lime." Which was such bollocks, but she knew enough about magic by now to know that wouldn't matter. She kept adding ingredients until the boiling mixture smelled like an industrial accident at Holland & Barrett. She added Luke's blood from the syringe and stirred it in. She was disturbed to find she felt affection even for the liquid. Now came the difficult bit. She'd only had a few lessons from Judith on the subject of projecting one's intent into matter through gesture and sound. She didn't know where to begin. If only she could just say, "and here's one I made earlier," like on the cooking shows. The three ways of empowering something were to make a sacrifice, use a sort of judo to fool the universe into doing something for you, or appeal to a higher power. Autumn didn't actually believe in the existence of any higher powers, but before she'd gained her extra senses, she had always relied on them as a metaphor, so now, as she made the basic hand movements she'd learned, she brought her own more nebulous icons of what she'd always regarded as he unconscious process in her own mind to bear on the working. The power of blood, which was meant to be mighty, would help.

It was going to have to be enough.

———

Judith was in hell.

That was the only conclusion she could come to. She was still aware, though it was a bit like being asleep. There was a cold darkness all around her, and she was falling. The fall was endless. So the cold kept chilling her to the point of fear, and her body kept jerking with the sudden realisation she was falling, over and over, and there was no stopping it.

She was falling through the architecture of the curse.

In other words, she was falling through a simulacrum of Arthur. She felt who he'd been and her love for her at every moment, enormously, through every pore of her skin.

She was in hell.

She was aware of her body, vaguely. She felt naked. Her eyes didn't seem to be working. Or there was nothing at all to see.

Robin, her old lover, had made this curse, all those years ago. His field of study had been necromancy, that bloody awful pit of dark clothes and graveyards and loving the dead. Whoever she'd ended up with as her sweetheart after Robin, the necromancer's trap had been set for them to fall into on their deathbed. Could you fight your way out of a curse? Had anyone ever been confronted by their just desserts and said "sod you" and got out of it?

Judith was lost. She didn't know where to begin. But she got the feeling she had forever to think about it.

———

Autumn lowered the mug from her lips, having drunk down the potion and felt, just for a moment, sad about . . . it was going, yes, it was actually going, she was losing the feeling, and that was making her sad! Sad but . . . no, why the hell would that make her sad? It was gone, that horrible feeling was gone, banished by her anti-love potion. It had worked. She was free of it, free to act. She slammed the mug down onto the table and pulled Lizzie to her, shaking in sheer relief. "Right," she said finally. "They took their best shot against all of us, whoever they are. But they didn't get me. Now let's see what we can do about you."

"Nothing to be done. Everything's fine. Let me get back to my work." Lizzie actually shook her head as she said the words, desperately denying them.

"Can you tell me why you've been trying to hurt yourself? What's this 'thing' someone wants you to do?"

Lizzie shook her head once again. "Nothing." She was looking ashen, as if whatever was wrong had increased in intensity, just in the time Autumn had been working here.

"No hurting!" called the ghost child.

What was the connection between the boy and Lizzie? Judith had called Autumn to warn her that something unusual might happen to her. Presumably her sudden passion for Luke had been one of the distortions in reality the old witch had been trying to sense. Was the child another? She had no idea how to get rid of it if it did turn out to be dangerous. Autumn looked at the clock. It was already past midnight. If Judith had, by some miracle, just been sulking at home all this time, she'd be long in her bed by now. But no, how likely was that? "Come on," she said to Lizzie. "Let's see what they've done to her." Whoever, she silently added, as they headed out, "they" were.

———

Standing outside Judith's house, Autumn could feel stark coldness radiating from one of the upper-floor rooms, beyond the cold in the street and the snow starting to fall around them. It was, she realised, a sensation she'd felt before, when passing Judith's house. It was only now she'd come here on the lookout for some kind of threat that it had become meaningful. She went to the door and paused. Okay, this was a bit like a police officer believing harm was being done inside a building right now, wasn't it? She looked to Lizzie and the ghost child beside her for an approval that was met only by Lizzie's look of agonised distraction. Okay then. Autumn took a run up and aimed a flying kick at the door.

She bounced off it and collapsed onto the pavement.

It turned out that doors were a bit harder to get through in real life than on TV. And of course Judith would have the sturdiest possible door.

"Did I really just see that?" a familiar voice said. Autumn looked up to see Judith's son, Shaun, heading over, the lights of his police car behind him. "Tell you what, let's say I didn't."

———————

It turned out that Shaun, aware that his mother hadn't been in touch for what was, even for her, a long time, had just come off shift, and had decided to come by to see if everything was all right. Autumn told him the truth about his Mum's absence from the shop in recent days, and Shaun used his own key to open the front door, which, worryingly, wasn't actually bolted. They stepped over a pile of mail to get in.

"Mum?" Shaun called up the stairs, his voice an aching compromise between professional and personal. He called twice again as he led the way up them, the former sound gradually taking over from the latter. He hadn't even asked why Lizzie was with them, and of course couldn't see the child, who was looking around himself in greater agitation the higher they climbed.

Shaun also obviously couldn't see, as they entered the bedroom, the strange sight that greeted Autumn and, she was sure from the look of surprise on her face, Lizzie. Alone in the room, there was a man, an old man, who was radiating the dark and the cold. He was standing by the window, his arms by his side, as if communing with something far away.

Shaun couldn't see him, but he reacted with alarm to the absence of Judith. He headed straight back out, presumably to mount a quick search of the rest of the rooms. Autumn and Lizzie stayed as the old man turned slowly toward them. "Amateurs," he said, in a voice meant only for them.

"She's not here," called Shaun from outside the room. "The place hasn't been lived in in days. Okay, that's it. I'm going back to the car to call it in."

They waited until they heard his steps recede down the stairs, then Autumn looked to the old man and realised she had now to say in deadly earnest a recurring joke from so many movies. "Who are you, and what have you done with Judith?"

The man laughed. "So she hasn't mentioned me? She wouldn't. I'm her husband, Arthur. Well, her ex. And what I've done has already given me a window on the world again, and is about to make me real, to set me free."

Autumn was desperately trying to get her head around what the relationship between Judith and this ghost had been. He looked like he'd been here for . . . had Judith really been living with this all this time? "Yeah, right," she said. "If we let it."

The man stepped toward them in anger. Autumn raised a finger in a basic protection gesture, the first thing

Judith had taught her, and he shrank back. His bark looked to be a lot bigger than his bite. "They promised," he whispered. "They got in touch from far away, asked me. I let them inside me, let them change me, they said it'd end up with me getting away from here, being able to go anywhere, becoming a whole person, all of my own."

Autumn wished she knew more about the nature of whatever this being was. The only way she could learn was to keep it talking. "It's pretty obvious something's trying to get into the town. Why would it care about you getting away?"

"They changed what's inside me. They set it up so that when she—"

"When she what?" He'd meant Lizzie, Autumn was sure.

The man shook his head, realising he'd said too much.

Judith had never liked Autumn using the word *experiment*, but maybe it was time for just that. "So it's about what's inside you? All right." Before the ghost could react, Autumn reached out and put her palm to the surface of its skin. She could feel such cold, such . . . wait a sec, why was the man suddenly smiling?

The sudden sidelong gravity wrenched her off her feet. She was hauled towards, no, into, Arthur with horrifying force. She threw out a hand, and grabbed, not Lizzie, as she'd intended, but whatever this oxygen tank thing was. But it lifted off the ground—

—and Autumn slammed into the ghost. And straight through it . . . into . . . where was she?! She screamed. The darkness was all around her, so dense she couldn't see. It felt like there was an infinite drop below her. She was . . . she realised she was still holding on to something with one hand. She flailed around with her free hand. She was being pulled downwards, and if she fell, she would fall forever.

She reached up, trying to blindly find with her other hand what one was still desperately clutching. She missed it. She tried again. The hand caught. She held on. She heaved. Something was coming for her from below, she realised. She felt, but couldn't see, something clutching, a hand, something like a human hand! Only it was so cold!

She broke the surface. She got her head out. She saw she'd been clinging to the oxygen tank, wedged against the end of the bed. She slapped one hand on it, then the other, and hauled herself out of the ghost, hand over hand, calling out all the time for Lizzie to help. Because if she fell back, if she didn't keep out of the reach of that hand, if she fell back, Lizzie was the only one left to—

Then Lizzie was there. She grabbed hold of Autumn and heaved.

Autumn fell onto the carpet. She looked back to what she'd crawled out of. Something was happening to

Arthur. The expression on his face was suddenly horrified. "No," he whispered. "No, no, I'm real. Please, let me be real. They're closing this end of it. But they promised!"

"Who promised?!" yelled Autumn.

"The couple. The family. From out there. They got me to do that to Judith. She's still inside. She'll always be inside now."

"Are you saying that's where Judith went, that she's in there?"

But Arthur couldn't answer. His face had contorted impossibly. A great sucking vortex had developed inside his chest, reaching for Autumn and Lizzie, only it couldn't reach far enough. Instead, it was consuming him. "No," he cried out forlornly. "No, I'm a person—!"

And suddenly he turned inside out like a sock and was gone into a twist of darkness, then nothing. Something slapped onto the carpet and vanished.

Autumn lay beside the oxygen tank, panting. She looked back to Lizzie. "The couple, the family. That's what he said. That's who's doing this to us. Do you have any idea who he's talking about?"

Lizzie helped her up, shaking her head, a look of distant horror on her face. Then all at once she relaxed. "Oh," she said. "Oh. Oh God. Thank God. It's gone."

"What?"

Lizzie started to laugh. "Autumn, you did it. Whatever

was trying to get across the borders, that was their way in, and somehow you closed it!" Lizzie grabbed her and held on. "Sorry I didn't help. Sorry I've been so weird. I was trying to hurt my hands, wasn't I? It was making me do that, I don't know why."

Autumn looked back to where Arthur had been. "But . . . I didn't do anything."

"Maybe disturbing the surface of that thing was enough to make it collapse?"

"Maybe." Autumn couldn't find it in her to share what felt like an odd and rather desperate sense of triumph on the part of her friend. There were still too many unanswered questions, too much still at stake. "Judith was in there. I think she's still in there. Even though the . . . door has gone."

"Oh no." Lizzie broke off and looked worried. "Can we get her back?"

Autumn sat down on the bed. "I don't know." She looked across at the ghost boy, who was still looking horrified at Lizzie. One thing above all was troubling her. If they'd just won . . . why was he still here?

Lizzie looked in the same direction and smiled sadly. "Looks like I've got a follower for life. Ah, well."

3

The Reverend Lizzie Blackmore, vicar of Lychford, spent December 23rd merrily attending Lychford's Christmas Fayre, and several people mentioned, as she went from stall to stall saying hello and distributing sweets, that they were pleased to see her smiling again, and were also a bit surprised that she hadn't mentioned, given her past form, that there was no "y" in "fair." On every occasion, with a laugh in her voice, she told them that fair was foul and foul was fair, which tended to get a slightly perplexed laugh in return. Mostly.

That day she also took Communion in the Nine Lives old people's home, and attended the rehearsal for the crib service. This involved the junior school and nursery children, so Lizzie had to put on an especially big smile when she saw Jamie Dunning in the audience. She was even called upon, as she ran the children through their parts, to put a doll in the manger. It turned out to be relatively easy not to think about what would happen the next time Jamie was in this building. There was, since Arthur had said those words to her in a different voice while Autumn was away, now something in her head to let her deal with all that. She wasn't compelled to hurt her hands, and that was a great relief. She could barely hear that small part of herself that was still free, screaming inside a distant room in her head. The actual crib service, since it was scheduled after the wedding on Christmas Eve, would of course never come to pass. But there was no point in letting the cat out of the bag about that.

Mind you, every time she looked at the ghost boy, things still got difficult. She wished she could be rid of him. Why was he still here? What was he for? He was terrified of the presence of the real Jamie Dunning, had tried helplessly to stop her from approaching him at every point.

As she locked the church that night, Lizzie wondered distantly what the town would look like after tomorrow, after Christmas Eve? She had been told that everything would be wonderful after the change, after the breaking down of the borders and the inversion. She had been told that Christmas would never come, that it would never come again. What would that be like?

There was only one more normal service to get through tomorrow, Holy Communion at 10 a.m., and then would come the wedding, and then it would all be over, for her, for Lychford, and for the world.

That evening, Autumn sat in the Plough, Christmas happening all around her, friends filling the pub with laughter and the literal warmth of bodies. Nothing could warm her. Despite Lizzie's assurances, and nothing setting alarms off in her own extra senses, she couldn't make herself believe the danger was over. She'd spent the day researching possibilities for how to rescue Judith. She hadn't even found the terms she needed to use to address the problem. If it were possible at all, it would take years, maybe a lifetime. She'd done everything she could to contact Finn, even replying to his email, but had gotten no response. Perhaps the fairies had decided the humans were on their own.

She looked up when the door opened. It was Shaun, in uniform, his face a picture of worry. She wished she could tell him the truth about Judith, so at least he'd stop searching in the real world, but no, she decided, she would only do that if she could also offer him hope. "I'm just stopping for a coffee," he said to Rob. "Another missing person tonight. Mum was the first one we've had in a decade, then two come along at once, maybe it isn't a coincidence."

"Who is it?" asked Autumn, intercepting him.

"A toddler," said Shaun. "He was at home in his room,

then he wasn't. I can't go into more detail than—"

"What's his name?"

"Jamie Dunning."

Those listening reacted, some of them knowing the parents. A mutter of worry went round the pub. But it was nothing compared to the sudden fear Autumn felt. She carefully put down her pint. "You're right," she said. "That's not a bloody coincidence."

———————

Autumn asked a few of the locals, found out where the Dunnings lived, and went into the Backs to find their semi-detached house. The police car lights identified it from quite a way off. She didn't know what she'd been hoping to see here. The best her extra senses could manage was a sense of . . . not quite a presence, just a shadow of something having been here. The shadow felt huge, painful, askew from everything, and utterly in hiding. Whatever it was a shadow of . . . Autumn felt a chill at the thought of facing the reality, of how big that would be. It reminded her, she realised, of whatever had grabbed for her in that endless darkness. "The couple, the family," she whispered under her breath. Those were the words Arthur had used.

She told herself that the mere fact that their enemy

remained in hiding, that they had tried to get rid of the stump that might indicate the most vague details about their nature, that they had closed off the literal loose end of Arthur, spoke of them still being somehow vulnerable. But that might not be the case for much longer.

Autumn got as close as she could, feeling the horror from the house more acutely as she did so. She could imagine it: looking in on a child's room to find it surprisingly empty, searching the house, at first bemused, then worried, then very quickly terrified. The impossibility of it would have hit them sideways. The height of that bedroom window off the ground. Everyday people shouldn't have things like this happen to them.

There was no way anyone was going to let her go inside to look more closely. And she was pretty certain there would be nothing more to find. Autumn turned and felt new determination as she headed for the Vicarage. Judith might be gone, but she and Lizzie were going to fight this thing. Autumn was going to go right now and get her.

Thank goodness Lizzie was back to her normal self.

───────────

Lizzie huddled in the kitchen with the lights off, listening to Autumn trying the doorbell for the fifth time. The ghost boy sat beside her, looking at her imploringly as always. "Why did I let you in?" she whispered. It would have been so much easier if she hadn't. Then she would be completely comfortable in what she was doing now. She could be comfortable. She was often comfortable. Except sometimes in the evenings, when she had nothing left to do and sleep still would not come. "They'd like me to get rid of you, but I can't. That look on your face keeps making me doubt."

The boy carefully reached up and climbed onto her to awkwardly sit on her lap, as if seeking any possible comfort.

"It's supposed to be Christmas," whispered Lizzie. "But now Christmas will never come." Christmas to her had always meant a little light, the light of the stable in the darkness of the winter. It was the hope that never died, but now it was going to. The hopes and fears of all the years are met in thee tonight, as the carol said. In the dark streets shineth . . . and now that light would be extinguished. There was a reason why people got depressed at Christmas, because it was the one point in the year where this flawed, selfish civilisation, rotten with money, still allowed itself to face infinite forgiveness, infinite compassion; people compared their situation to the parade of home and hearth and tinsel that had been draped over that fact and instead of finding hope they despaired.

Infinite forgiveness, infinite compassion, all gone. A surrender to despair.

All she had to do was get up and open the front door, and let Autumn in, like one day, so long ago it felt, she'd been brave enough to let this boy in. Come on, Lizzie, said a different voice, a voice like a father, somewhere. Come on. It's not too much for you. There's no such thing as too much for you.

She pushed down on her feet and rose slowly, her back against the cupboards. The ghost boy looked excitedly up at her, hope on his face for the first time.

She took a step across the kitchen, everything they'd put in her brain screaming at her now to stop. Oh, they must be afraid of Autumn. What she and Autumn could do together. A sudden crippling headache turned into physical pain, racking her back and chest. What these things couldn't do, she told herself, putting one foot in front of the other, was kill her. They needed her. So she would walk herself forward into death if they pushed it that far. She wouldn't give up before they did. She'd walk right into death and away from all this and she would beat them like that if she couldn't do it now like this.

The ghost boy stepped with her, looking up eagerly at her, holding her hand.

She made it into the hallway, and realised blood was now running freely from her nose. It was like hangover on hangover was being thrown into her head. Her vision was distorting with the pain. She stumbled at the door, and as her lungs started to contort in some sort of shock, she managed to use the last of her breath to rip out the security chain and heave the door open.

"Autumn!" she cried out.

But there was nobody there. The pain had been roaring in her ears so much, she hadn't noticed when the doorbell ringing had stopped. She stood there for a moment, having given her all, staring into the darkness that had no light in it. Beside her, she was aware of the ghost boy making huge horrified sobs. The pain suddenly fell from her like the punchline to a sick joke.

She collapsed beside the ghost and held him as the rain started to fall on them both.

————————

Autumn couldn't bring herself to stay up late watching the lovely old movies they put on the telly at this time of year. She had none of that Christmas Eve tomorrow feeling which she'd never quite lost from childhood. She was sure she wouldn't feel right again, not until she'd found some way to discover what had happened to Judith, some way to find the lost child.

She fell on her bed, exhausted, intending to get just a

quick nap before going back to her research, and was surprised when she woke to light and the sounds of morning. She lay there, wishing some insight had come to her,
in her . . . actually, it kind of had. What had Judith said
about the ghost child, that a doppelgänger could be an attempt to stop the thing it was warning against from happening? Either that or it was trying to make it happen.
And it kept saying "no hurting," as if it didn't want to be
hurt. Well, if harm coming to the real boy was what it was
warning against, it didn't seem like its presence was a self-
fulfilling prophecy, given that it was haunting Lizzie. . . .
Unless it was Lizzie who had kidnapped the real . . . no,
of course she hadn't! Though Autumn wished she knew
where her friend had got to last night, because perhaps
there was something still just a bit wrong going on there.
So if the ghost boy was trying to *help* his real self, *then*
why haunt Lizzie? No idea. And it wasn't as if the boy
himself could tell her . . . unless . . .

"Oh," she said aloud. "Oh. How do you power up a
ghost?"

———

Autumn ran into her laboratory, still in her dressing
gown, and started grabbing ingredients. This, your basic passing on of power to something or someone,

wasn't difficult, this was the basics. This was what Lizzie would call a blessing. She would need, again, either the judo or the appeal to a higher power or the sacrifice, but, oh, this was going to be the tough bit, that little ghost was really lacking the ability to convey much of a message. He'd need a lot of support added to him, her own rather academic internal icons weren't going to do it on their own, and this time she didn't have the power of good old-fashioned blood to give the whole thing a bit of *oomph.*

She really needed a sacrifice. What could she put into this working that was important enough to her, that she would acutely feel the loss of?

Her phone rang. She saw who it was, and was surprised to the point of astonishment, but relieved to these days be able to answer calmly. Of course, if he were calling because he realised she'd stolen his blood, then she was just going to end the call. "Luke. Hi."

"Hi." He sounded like he was being really careful. Of course he was.

"Listen, I'm sorry about the other night—"

"I don't actually remember much after you arrived." Yes, thought Autumn, that would be the effect of those sleeping herbs. "I must confess, I did wonder if I dreamt all that. Am I right in thinking you . . . brought a vicar?"

"I brought my friend Lizzie."

"What did we talk about? I remember you were trying to . . . explain?"

"You were kind enough to listen."

"I remember you making sense. You sound like you're doing okay again now."

He meant with her mental health, Autumn realised. This guy thought she was ill, but was actually willing to engage with that. "I am. Sorry again."

"I'm taking part in the search through the woods today. You know, the police are getting a lot of local people together to look for . . . well, nobody's saying what they're looking for, but we all know—"

"You haven't gone home?" He'd told her about getting back to his friends on their drunken night together, which now seemed like it had been centuries ago.

"No, I've been putting it off . . . because of you. Because I really liked that evening and I can deal with the . . . health issues, and . . . what I'm going to be doing today, it makes you think about what's important, doesn't it? Especially on Christmas Eve. So I was wondering if . . . maybe you'd like to meet up for a coffee, after, or after I get back in the New Year, and—?"

Autumn had closed her eyes. She so wanted this. She so wanted this to be the ending of her Christmas rom com. But he didn't actually know what he was signing up for. Maybe the loneliness, the burden that Judith had borne, unspoken, was the sacrifice you made to protect something you cared about. Like this was going to be her sacrifice now. "I'm sorry," she said. "You're brilliant, but I can't see you anymore." She clicked off the phone and made the gesture of adding the sacrifice to the working, and as she started to brew the potion she added to it her tears.

————————

After she was finished, Autumn stumbled to the door of the shop and swung it open, letting the clear air of a crisp winter morning in and the heat of the brewing process out. She stood there on the threshold, wiping her face on her sleeve. She could hear the church bells ringing for what must be . . . she checked her watch . . . Lizzie's first service of the day would already be over, so that must be the wedding. She felt dizzy from having put so much of her own energy into the working. Stupid girl. What had she hoped to achieve, anyway?

She realised, as she wiped the tears from her eyes, that a small figure was standing on the pavement across the road. The ghost boy was looking at her like she was his last, desperate hope. "It's okay," she called, quickly. "It's all going to be all right!" He stepped slowly across the road, ignoring the car that passed through him and caused Autumn to yell, and finally stopped in front of her. "Come in," she said. "Please."

———————

Autumn didn't have much experience with children, and this being a ghost child, she didn't feel able to offer him a biscuit. She closed the shop door behind him and squatted down to his level. "What's your name?"

"Sort of . . . Jamie."

He was definitely able to communicate more easily. Probably better than the real child. "Do you know where Jamie . . . the real Jamie . . . is right now?"

"I'm in a big white car."

Autumn's mind raced. That was a useful detail, but she needed a lot more if she were going to somehow find a way to tell this to Shaun. "Can you see where you are?" The boy nodded. "What's around you?"

"People in the car. People in suits. Flowers on suits."

Flowers on suits? Like clowns?

"Men with flowers on suits. Big white dress."

Autumn stood up. That sounded like . . . and a line of connections suddenly raced through her mind. The couple. The family. No hurting! Why had this boy haunted Lizzie? Lizzie had wanted to hurt her hands, stop herself doing "the thing" which had looked like . . . stabbing.

"The wedding," she whispered to herself. "Oh, dear God, it's the wedding!"

———

Lizzie stood at the door of the church, welcoming all the shapes and shadows that burst and fluttered past her without a word. They would be unseen to the everyday people of Lychford, she was sure. What would happen if she didn't welcome them into the church? Well, that was why she needed to welcome them. The doubts of the night were behind her. Thankfully, as she'd been getting ready, the ghost boy had vanished, too. Hopefully the real thing was being calmed about the matter of his fate. No, no, she wouldn't listen to the part of her that was screaming. She had to dab at her nose every now and then to stop the blood, but that was only to be expected. The groom was already inside the church, of course, even bigger than before and standing at a strange angle, standing with his family, filling the place and changing the space, and preventing all the things this church would normally be. He'd shaken hands with her, and his hand had been so cold.

The happy couple had been so clever. The wedding had been so well arranged. Jamie would be brought in right at the last moment, she'd been told. Any people who thought for some reason to look in on the wedding would be discouraged by the presence of the ushers, and Derek of the hidden face, who was stalking the edges of the church, waiting for victims as a best man should. Hopefully he'd be back in place when it came time to hand over the rings. The organist, who was now playing clashing, impossible chords, had been brought in from elsewhere. The bell ringers—who were now causing the bells to leap in frenzy on their ropes—had been, too. None of her usual folk who might have seen what was happening were here. Everything had been thought of.

Ah. Here came the bride. Everyone else had gotten inside in time. Emma was getting out of a white limo at the bottom of the path and was progressing through the lych-gate, her white dress and train somehow . . . hissing as they made contact with the ground, and there was just the smallest trace of smoke rising into the air as the dress ignited the last few dead leaves with her passing. Behind her walked her maids of honour, now visible as many-faceted things, their eyes reflecting glory. In her hands, the bride carried, because she was impossibly strong, the struggling small figure of Jamie Dunning, who'd been dressed in a little suit of his own, with a buttonhole, even. The light in the eyes of the maids, Lizzie knew, would stop those who'd idly gathered to watch the bride go in from seeing the little captive, from seeing that anything was amiss.

Lizzie, her teeth grinding, bowed her head as the bride approached, and was delighted to hear her laughter and feel the warmth of her breath on her face. "Is he waiting?" she asked.

"He is waiting," whispered Lizzie.

"Is the knife washed and prepared?"

Lizzie tried to make herself look down at Jamie, who'd started screaming, but she couldn't. "The knife is washed and prepared."

"And are you prepared to use it?"

Lizzie managed, just, to stop herself from replying, but her head, held in a vicelike grip of muscle control, was forced to nod.

———

Autumn had gotten dressed quickly and had gathered what little she could think of that might be useful for protection, with the ghost boy watching, desperately urging her on. Should she call Shaun? No, she should go to find him. He'd always known and accepted a little of what his mother had done. Maybe Autumn stood a chance of convincing him. If she couldn't, then she was going to have to do this alone. Well, apart from the boy, and what could he contribute? As she locked the shop behind her and stepped out into the street, he followed her. "No hurting?" he asked plaintively.

"I hope not," said Autumn. "But—" No, she didn't want to say aloud that she had no idea what she could do to stop this.

Lizzie stood in front of the pulpit, the bride and groom kneeling in front of her, looking out at a bizarre congregation that filled the pews like a shifting sea of light. Sea was right, she thought; she could feel it beating against the barriers, eager to soon get in. When it did, they would all be lost among it. That, she told herself sternly, was a good thing. Jamie was being held by three . . . she had no idea what they were. He hadn't stopped screaming. Derek and the father of the bride stood nearby, the latter flickering in anticipation. The two statues were in place, at odd positions inside the church, their shadows fixing everything where it had to be. Lizzie began reading the words that had been handed to her, the three poems that would prepare the shape of the changes brought by the sacrifice. It would all be over soon.

Autumn tried at the local police station, which had a

small queue of volunteers at the door and a calm police officer at the desk, dealing with the public end of the operation. Shaun, she was told by those in the queue, would be out in the woods somewhere, with the search. Autumn considered for a moment how long she had, and what help any everyday person might be, even if he brought the whole Gloucestershire constabulary with him. Then she decided. It was going to have to be just her and the boy.

She marched across the marketplace, past the Christmas tree with the brass band playing, and up the road that led to the church, as excited families with children went past her, heading out for last-minute shopping at shops that were lit up and decorated. The boy walked with her, looking nervous but urging her on. Whatever the consequences of what was going on in that church were meant to be, would this lot be aware of them either way?

She looked up at the tower of St. Martin's as she approached and saw that the neon star now shone. . . . Her extra senses saw it was shining black, somehow, a glittering darkness that was pulsing, increasing, pushing against the sky. The shadows that flashed from it onto the churchyard made the frost hiss.

She walked up the path, aware that she was probably going to her death. Only the anger at what this lot had done to Judith, the knowledge that Lizzie was inside the building, let her keep going. Just a few days ago, her biggest worry had been that she was working her way through a list of rom-com clichés, but now... She increased her speed as she headed for the big wooden doors, ignoring what her senses were telling her about the sheer weight of a terrifying presence inside, and slammed them open to rush into the church. "Stop the wedding!" she yelled.

As everything in this... horrifyingly alien mass of things slowly turned to look at her, Autumn realised she might not have entirely escaped those rom-com clichés after all. But she had no time to think about that. There was Lizzie, and there was the real Jamie Dunning, both standing by the font, and Lizzie... had her arm raised and a knife in her hand, and she was holding Jamie with the other hand and he was screaming!

Autumn in that same moment made eye contact with Lizzie and saw such pain and helplessness in her friend's eyes. She ran at her, the ghost boy yelling in fear beside her. She was aware as she did so that suddenly smoke was pouring from her bag and from her pockets. The protective charms she'd brought along: this place was dissolving them!

Lizzie screamed herself as she swung the knife.

Autumn leapt forward and caught her wrist. She was

aware of a strange noise rising from the building all around her. She was sure it was some otherworldly version of laughter. The bride and groom ... Autumn didn't want to think about what they looked like, and now they'd gotten to their feet and were standing over the two of them, enjoying the spectacle. "No hurting!" cried the ghost boy. His real-life version was sobbing too much to form words.

Lizzie, her expression desperate, was using all her strength and some that came from beyond her to force the blade down. Autumn realised that she was wasn't going to be able to stop her. The sharp point of the knife was heading for the boy's throat. Lizzie had him by the hair. "Lizzie, stop, please, this isn't you!" But she could see from Lizzie's face that she knew, and she was already doing everything she could to stop herself. "What can I do? Lizzie, what can we do to help you?!"

With agonising slowness, Lizzie managed to turn her head. It was obviously something whatever was controlling her didn't want. She was looking, Autumn realised, straight at the ghost boy. She was wanting something ... from him? Autumn looked back to him. He was nodding, encouraging her ... reaching out to her.

He was moving so slowly, as if something was holding him back. Autumn was losing her grip on Lizzie's wrist. The forces acting through her friend were just too strong.

Oh God. Oh God . . . Autumn realised she was going to have to take an enormous gamble. Let every aspect of every archetype inside her be onside now, because . . .

She heaved Lizzie back, and in the same moment grabbed the ghost boy, using all the willpower she had to actually be able to lay hands on him. She felt him cooperate with that. As Lizzie leapt forward again, knife in hand, to finish her bloody task—

Autumn threw the ghost boy at her.

Lizzie reflexively stabbed in the air at the phantom. The ghost . . . disintegrated. Its vapour shot into every orifice of Lizzie's face and vanished into her.

The only sound now was the screaming of the real boy as he desperately looked up at Lizzie, wondering what she was about to do. She still had the knife in her hand. Autumn realised: the otherworldly laughter had stopped.

The groom stepped forward, a huge shadow that made Autumn cry out as it fell across her.

Lizzie turned to face him and with one reflexive movement broke the knife over her knee. "How dare you bring this to my father's house?" she whispered.

Autumn had never been so relieved to see her friend angry.

The creature lunged for the boy, but Autumn grabbed him out of the way and leapt back so they could both stand behind Lizzie, who was now shouting out words of what must be liturgy. As the groom reached for them, Lizzie made the cross gesture of blessing.

The groom staggered backwards, swatting the air.

The church physically rocked.

Autumn fell as she felt the ocean of fury slam itself all at once against the boundaries. She clambered to her feet to see Lizzie holding back the groom, and the bride now beside him, with gesture and words and sheer anger. Where had she gotten all this energy from?

The bride and groom were once more forced back. Lizzie turned and started frantically blessing the congregation, marking out the boundaries of the church in gesture. The beings screamed, the tide slammed backwards against the far wall, and rushed forward at them. Autumn cried out as the bride and groom swept toward them at the head of the mass.

She saw at the last second what the groom was trying to do. His extraordinarily cold hand reached out impossibly across so many different directions at once, and it landed on Jamie's arm. Lizzie turned, reached out at the same instant Autumn did, completing her blessing with a shout.

But that shout made the tide turn, in one motion. Exactly as the groom must have expected. The whole congregation, the bride and groom with it, that whole mass of impossibility shot back towards the door, stretching

Autumn's vision with a blur of painful gravity.

Jamie's fingers missed theirs. He shot away with the tide.

The big doors slammed. The church was whole again. The forces from beyond had gone.

But they had taken Jamie with them.

Lizzie leapt to her feet. "Come on!" she shouted. She sprinted off towards the door.

Autumn heaved herself to her feet and followed. "Where will they take him?!"

"I don't know!" They burst out of the church together and saw a blur of something snapping into the white limousine at the bottom of the path, which then suddenly started up and began to accelerate away.

They raced to the bottom of the path. Autumn saw Mick the builder getting out of his van by the cashpoint on the other side of the road. "Mick," she shouted. "Jamie Dunning is in that car!"

Mick took one look at her, realised she was serious, and ran back to his van. Autumn and Lizzie got to the sliding side door just as he started the engine. "They don't have a turnoff that way for about a mile!" he called. "We can catch up with them. One of you call the police."

Autumn was already doing so. At least, she thought, as they took a scary turn out into the traffic, horn blaring, here was something for Shaun to go after. She called the number she'd seen on posters asking for information, and got straight through to someone who seemed far more willing to believe her when she put Lizzie on the line. Lizzie spoke quickly but very precisely, making up on the spot a story about seeing Jamie with someone in her church, who'd fled when she challenged them. It would do, Autumn supposed. Lizzie switched off the phone when the call was over. "We've been told not to pursue them, to leave it to the police," she said to Mick.

"Yeah, not doing that." Ahead Autumn could see the limo, glimpsed through the trees as it took the curves at speed. But then, suddenly, it veered off the road.

"Oh no," said Lizzie.

But as they themselves turned the corner, it became clear that the car hadn't crashed. It had gone straight through a fence and was speeding up across a ploughed field, the mud flying from its wheels. It was heading, Autumn realised, for the woods. "How the hell did it do that?" said Mick. "I can try to take us up there, but the ditch—"

"Stop here," said Lizzie. As Mick brought the van to a screeching halt, she was already unbuckling her safety belt, and Autumn followed suit.

"You stay here, tell the police where—" began Mick, who was also clambering out.

"No, you do that," shouted Lizzie, and was out and

running before he could argue. Autumn made sure with a look that he was going to stay put and ran after her. Ahead, the limo had stopped, and three figures were running for the tree line. "They're heading for the paths that the police won't find," panted Lizzie. "Only we can follow them there."

"Why do they still want Jamie? If the sacrifice has been messed up—"

"They must be able to do something with him. Only the two of them left; the others must have retreated over the border. Maybe if they make a sacrifice there, they can at least weaken the boundary enough to let them in. They were going to get the whole thing in one go, but if they do it this way they'll have to fight for it."

"You did great in there."

"I did bloody awfully. I should never have let them—"

"You didn't let them do anything. They did this to you." The figures had vanished into the trees ahead. Autumn and Lizzie got there moments later, on the paths only they could walk, and Autumn found she recognised where they were. "If they're heading for their own border, surely we won't even be able to see that?"

"All we've ever seen," called Lizzie as she ran on down the path, her breath misting on the air, "is the one border, when Judith had us walk it. Maybe that stands in all directions."

They reached a conjunction of paths. Autumn re-alised, at the same moment as Lizzie evidently did, that there were several different directions they could go from here to get to the boundary. "Which is the quickest way?"

"Bit of a toss-up. Damn it."

As they looked around for any sign of which way the couple might have gone, Autumn realised she could hear something familiar, a long way off. It was something she associated with . . . well, once it had been fear, but now it was confusion . . . it was a high, repetitive, six-note strain, followed by a recurring three-note summons. It was the music, the music Finn often played! "This way!" she said, and sped off down one of the paths.

After turning left and right for a few minutes, follow-ing the music, they burst into a clearing. What was nor-mally invisible, Autumn realised, even to them, was now horribly apparent. This must be the border itself, one side of the clearing wildly fluctuating between the scene of the everyday trees beyond and . . . several different land-scapes, one of which she recognised as the land of fairy. That was gorgeous, too gorgeous, but some of what she saw in those other moments . . . she wanted to close her eyes. But she would not. Because, above and beyond all that, here they were; the big thing and the little thing, now returned to their human guises, "Alan" and "Emma." Alan held, in one enormous hand, Jamie Dunning. His other hand held a Stanley knife, up against the boy's throat.

"What are you?" asked Lizzie.

"We own this land," said Emma. "We were here millions of years before you people in your swarms, with your weird religions, walked over from the continent, bringing your fairies with you. We're tired of living in the cracks. We don't like being banished. We want back what's ours."

"And that's worth the life of a child?" asked Autumn.

"Course it is! These 'lives' of yours exist only in time and come to a stop anyway," sniffed Emma. "Bunch of perverts."

Autumn was wondering what they could possibly do next. These two were clearly waiting for something, perhaps for when their forces would rally and appear in one of the many landscapes that were appearing in rotation behind them. While she was thinking that, she found herself watching those many landscapes and saw in one of them . . . but then it was gone again. "Keep them talking," she whispered to Lizzie.

Lizzie did so. "So the changing of the seasons, moments like Christmas, are nothing to you? It's all just . . . now?"

"Much the better system," said Alan.

Autumn watched again as the landscapes cycled past, and this time she saw it clearly. Approaching the boundary was some sort of army. All she could see were glimpses of light on sword and shield, but the way she couldn't quite see what was carrying the weapons was deeply familiar to her. These were the fairies, the army of the Summerland, going to war. And there, she could clearly see, because he must have let her see, there was Finn at the front of them, a look of calm determination on his face she'd never seen, and there beside him, with a sword the size of a small tree . . . oh. *Oh.* "You're going to want to start negotiating," she said to the couple.

"No," said Emma patiently, "because nothing can get across the boundary unless we allow it. Fixing that was pretty high on our to-do list."

"Yeah, but things can still go through the other way, right?" Autumn stepped forward until she was looking up at Alan. His size and presence terrified her. She was only going to get a moment to do this, and again, if she got it wrong, a child would die.

"Well of course they can. Or our forces would never have been able to fall back. Even now they'll be regrouping, ready for—"

Autumn had just seen out of her peripheral vision, as the landscapes cycled back to the land of fairy, and the army was here now, and right here, up against the boundary—

She leapt at Alan, caught him low with her head, under

his centre of gravity, and pushed.

He staggered back, bemused more than anything, effortlessly keeping hold of the screaming child. He stepped back to steady himself.

He stepped over the border.

"Hoi," said a voice from behind him.

Alan spun to look.

Which was the exact moment Judith Mawson swung at him a fairy sword the size of a small tree.

The sword connected with Alan's neck. His head flew off like a coconut knocked from a shy. Autumn felt but did not see a much bigger event, the visible beheading a metaphor for a death that was harder to comprehend, a mystical sundering that could only have been completed by a weapon like that sword.

The body fell to the ground.

Jamie Dunning fell beside it, yelling in fear.

Judith inclined her head to Autumn. "How's that for customer satisfaction, then?"

"You're alive," said Lizzie, astonished.

"Just about," said Judith. "I'll tell you later. Now push her across and all." She indicated Emma. Autumn realised the boundary had stopped cycling. Whatever power had made it do that had been wrested away from the couple when Alan had died. Finn had squatted down beside Jamie and was reaching out to him with birdsong and a smile, the most human she had ever seen him, while the army behind him continued to seethe with angry intent. Autumn looked back to Lizzie, and realised she was actually hesitating.

———

The Reverend Lizzie Blackmore had come to this place with nothing but a desire for justice in her mind, a righteous rage at what these two had done to her, at what they'd nearly made her do to a child.

But she didn't trust that feeling in herself. She never had.

"No," she said. "Put her on trial if you like—"

"That's not how we do things," said Finn from the other side of the boundary, quite gently. He was still holding Jamie, making sure the boy didn't look at the corpse.

"Don't piss this lot off, Lizzie," said Judith. "They're here with a good fraction of the big lad's power. They could just walk in and take her."

"Then they'll have to come through me," said Lizzie, stepping in front of Emma. She gathered that the big lad must be Finn's father, about whom Autumn had told her enough to know that she'd just done something really stupid.

"I don't want your forgiveness," hissed Emma.

"Tough," said Lizzie. She turned back to address Finn, Judith, and the army. "If I give her up to you to be killed, if I don't do everything I can to stop that, then midnight tonight won't mean anything anyway. Not for me. And so this lot will have made the difference they were after. In one person, anyway."

Autumn looked hard at her, then sighed and stepped up to join her. "Me, too," she said. "Though that doesn't mean I think it was wrong to cut his head off."

"That is a bit different," agreed Lizzie. "He was going to kill Jamie."

Judith looked them both up and down. "Idiots," she sighed. She stuck the enormous sword into the ground and turned to confide in Finn.

Emma leapt for the cover of the trees. Before Lizzie could react, an enormous sound roared past her head. The tree beside Emma sang with the impact of something like lightning and exploded.

Lizzie blinked at the light and Emma had gone. She had escaped back to her own world. Damn it.

Lizzie turned back to see Judith had her hand on Finn's arm. He was glowering at her, while still smiling at Jamie with the same face. She had, Lizzie realised, spoiled his aim. "They'll be back, you know," he said. "That'll be your fault."

"No," said Lizzie. "Now it'll be theirs."

———————

Jamie Dunning was eventually prised out of Finn's care, the fairy having asked if he wanted to stay in their lands a while, to which Judith, Autumn, and Lizzie together had quickly answered for the boy in the sternest negative terms. Finn had said they were disrespecting the cultural values of his people, and had added, more seriously, that he and Autumn had issues now; all three of them did. They had frustrated the will of his father, and brought future danger to his kingdom. As the fairies flickered away into the setting sun of late afternoon, taking that dirty great sword and the body of Alan with them, Autumn found that she really couldn't give two hoots about what Finn's dad wanted, and flicked two fingers in their direction. "And a Merry Christmas to you, too, you ungrateful sods."

"We could," said Judith, leading the toddler along the path with one finger in his hand as the early afternoon darkness closed in, "have ended up with them owing us a favour." She considered for a moment. "Which might have been worse."

"How did you get out?" asked Autumn. "How did you get here?"

Ahead of them, at the point where their path met the paths of the real world, they could see a group of police officers, locals, and dogs moving frantically at an angle to them. In a moment the four of them would emerge into their sight. "You get the lad home," said Judith. "I'll tell you down the Plough tonight." She took Jamie's hand and put it in Lizzie's.

"No hurting," said Jamie, proudly. Which made Lizzie smile.

"No," said Autumn. "Judith, you lead him out and be the hero. Go on."

Judith coughed a laugh. "You can't be the one who takes heads and be the hero, too. You'll learn that, my apprentice." And without another word, she turned and trudged off in another direction.

Lizzie picked up Jamie, and walked forward into shouts and cries of relief and, growing as more and more people arrived and the news spread, applause.

Autumn watched it all bounce off Lizzie like rain. But when Mike and Allison Dunning were called and ran forward to embrace their child, at least the Reverend allowed herself a smile.

Epilogue

Judith took a long drink from her pint, then set it down. The three of them had found a nook in the back bar of the hugely crowded Plough Inn where they couldn't be overheard. "I suppose," she said, "I'll have to start grieving properly now. So I've got that to look forward to."

"You lived with the ghost of Arthur," said Autumn, "all that time." She'd also got a pint, but Lizzie, who had Midnight Mass to begin preparing for in ten minutes, was on coffee. They'd both had to run the gauntlet of locals, Mick included, offering to buy them drinks. Mick himself had already benefitted from the generosity of those who'd heard he'd been part of the rescue effort. Shaun, hours earlier, had taken the (almost entirely fictitious) testimony of Lizzie and Autumn, to pass on to what Autumn assumed would be a meaningless search for the perpetrators. While doing so, he'd taken, first to his joy, then his annoyance, a phone call from his mum, who, Autumn judged by his reactions, told him she'd been off in London Christmas shopping. She gathered he'd been making some sort of fuss about her being away.

"You get used to things," said Judith.

"You should have told us," said Lizzie.

"Why? What would you have done? Apart from moping and telling me I should mope, too."

Autumn sighed. "How did you get out?"

"I heard you screaming when you fell into Arthur, too. That gave me a reference point, a way to start working out where I was. You giving more power to that ghost, that also had a bit of me in him, that was like a beacon, too. The structure of the curse was still there. It was powered by undead animals a certain someone had buried in the woods. Once I could see the shape of it, I gathered up all the power I could from . . . the sort of recording of the real Arthur that was in there; he couldn't help but help me, and I found my way out along the shape of the curse, to a real place, or at least as real as the borderlands are. I couldn't come out on our side of the border, so I decided to come out in fairy instead. Where I immediately had a word with the big lad. Hence them loaning me the Sword of a Billion Heads, I think it were called. Billion and one now." She laughed again, a very dark laugh.

"The sheer knowledge it took to do that," said Autumn. "Bloody hell."

Judith gestured in Lizzie's direction. "She managed to save herself without knowing a thing."

"How did I do that?" Lizzie looked puzzled.

"You kept giving your energy to the ghost lad. By letting him in, letting him follow you, trusting him. Without knowing it, you were storing it like in a savings account, protecting it by hiding it in the glitch in the worlds, so you could use it later."

"The light in the darkness," said Lizzie. "The hope out of nothing."

"Are you carrying on an old conversation again?" said Judith, clearly disapproving of the application of poetry to magic.

"Yeah," said Lizzie. "You could say that."

"Oh, hey." Autumn turned at the sound of the familiar voice. Standing in the entrance to the back bar was Luke. Autumn found herself without the power of speech. After all she'd gone through today, this was beyond her ability to cope with. "I heard what you two did. Are you okay?"

"She was a complete hero," said Lizzie, before Autumn could self-deprecate. "It was all down to her."

"You two go and talk in the front bar," said Judith. "Me and the vicar have got matters of high import to discuss."

Annoyed as she was by that blatant bit of social engineering on Judith's part, Autumn did as she was told, and let herself be bought drinks, and told Luke the (almost but not quite so much entirely fictitious) story of what had happened. She could only tell him, when he asked about her apparent former desire that he go away, that things with her were always complicated, that she'd thought she'd been doing something good, and actually had been, but sometimes doing something like that seemed to lead to good things in return that were totally undeserved. Autumn was nudged by Lizzie as she went off to arrange Midnight Mass, and she found herself, as the hour approached and they'd both had a few, with Luke under that mistletoe in the middle of the front bar. He looked as surprised as she was. He put a hand to the side of her face. "Merry Christmas," he said.

And it turned out, in the end, that Autumn really didn't mind getting to the end of that list of rom-com clichés.

———

Lizzie looked out at her considerably larger than normal congregation for Midnight Mass, including two relieved parents and their sleeping toddler. The crib service had been cancelled this year, due to the unexpected circumstance of the vicar becoming a local hero. People had wondered if this service would go ahead. Lizzie had told them that her not missing this had been the whole point of her day. "Welcome all wonders in one sight," she said, "eternity shut in a span. Summer in winter, day in night, heaven in earth and God in man. Great little one whose all-embracing birth brings earth to heaven, stoops heaven to earth."

She hadn't known what her sermon was going to be about until, just before joining Autumn and Judith down the pub, she'd done some random research. Tonight she was going to talk about the values underlying Christmas, and how the famous writer of what was often thought of as a sarcastic festive hit had declared he loved Christmas, but that he was actually protesting how commercialised it had become.

She wondered though, looking at the relative youth of this lot, how many of them would have heard of Greg Lake.

About the Author

© Lou Abercrombie, 2015

PAUL CORNELL is a writer of science fiction and fantasy in prose, comics, and television, one of only two people to be Hugo Award nominated for all three media. A *New York Times* #1 bestselling author, he's written *Doctor Who* for the BBC, *Wolverine* for Marvel, and *Batman and Robin* for DC. He's won the BSFA Award for his short fiction and an Eagle Award for his comics, and he shared in a Writer's Guild Award for his TV work.

TOR·COM

Science fiction. Fantasy. The universe.

And related subjects.

*

More than just a publisher's website, *Tor.com*
is a venue for **original fiction, comics,** and
discussion of the entire field of SF and fantasy,
in all media and from all sources. Visit our site
today — and join the conversation yourself.

11/16